Also by Bruce Jay Friedman

Steambath (a play)
The Dick
Scuba Duba (a play)
Black Angels (stories)
A Mother's Kisses
Far from the City of Class (stories)
Stern

aBOUT
HarrY
TOWns

ABOUT HARRY TOWNS

Bruce Jay Friedman

ALFRED A. KNOPF
NEW YORK
1974

THIS IS A BORZOI BOOK
PUBLISHED BY ALFRED A. KNOPF, INC.

Copyright © 1969, 1970, 1971,
1972, 1973, 1974 by Bruce Jay Friedman

All rights reserved under International and Pan-American
Copyright Conventions. Published in the United States by
Alfred A. Knopf, Inc., New York, and simultaneously in Canada
by Random House of Canada Limited, Toronto. Distributed by
Random House, Inc., New York.

Portions of this book in a slightly different form previously
appeared in: *Playboy, Esquire,* and *Harper's Magazine.*

Library of Congress Cataloging in Publication Data

Friedman, Bruce Jay (date)   About Harry Towns.

                                         I.   Title.
PZ4.F8988Ab   [PS3556.R5]   813'.5'4   73–20762
                                ISBN 0–394–48178–X

Manufactured in the United States of America

First Edition

For George Krupp
and Robert Gottlieb

① JUST BaCK From THE COaST

At the time Apollo 11 took off for the moon, Harry Towns was in a reclining chair beside the pool at a Beverly Hills hotel, taking advantage of the first stretch of absolutely perfect weather he had run into in Los Angeles. On his previous trips, whenever it rained or was generally dismal, someone would say, "I don't understand. It's never done this before, this time of year." When something went wrong in Los Angeles, people tended to say it was the first time in memory it had ever happened that way. Things didn't go wrong that often. And there was certainly nothing to quibble about on this trip. A poolside philosopher, sitting next to Towns, said the swimming area at the hotel was probably the only enclave in the world in which people were totally oblivious of that trip to the moon. "That's because they probably haven't figured out a way to make money on it," the fellow said. Towns was thinking about the moon landing, but in the cool, constant L. A. sun, he could not honestly say it was pressing heavily on his mind. He was winding up his West Coast trip, milking the last juice out of it, and had it worked out so that he would stay slightly involved in the flight while in California and then see the actual landing on the moon when he was back in New York. His son was away at summer camp and had asked Towns to round up at least twenty copies of the *New York Times* edition that reported the landing. "Can you imagine what copies of the Wright brothers newspaper would be worth today?" he had asked. Towns thought his son was very enterprising and made a sacred pledge to round up the papers, although secretly he decided ten was plenty for the kid. Meanwhile, he was busy loving California. He had made some short probing trips to the Coast before, barely taking time to get unpacked, but this had been a one-month visit and it was as though some of the seeds he had scattered earlier had come into flower. People fell in love with California by the carload, but he wondered if anyone had experienced quite the love affair he was having with the state. Did anyone love the orange juice as much as he did? It knocked him on his ear every time he had a fresh glass of it in the morning. The same went for the lettuce. Whoever heard of lettuce that had so much bite and spank and crunch to it? He loved the salad oils and so far he had not come across a wine that didn't taste marvelous. He began to guzzle it like water and that was another thing: he never got drunk in Los Angeles no matter how much he had to drink. It was like being in a super-rarified health simulator that didn't let you get drunk. In the way of many New Yorkers, he had spoken a bit too fondly of New York restaurants on the plane to L. A. and, by implication, had been a bit disdainful of restaurants anywhere else. The fellow next to him, who had been quite jovial up to that point, suddenly dropped his voice, and in a surprisingly ominous, almost cruel tone, asked, "Which restaurants did you go to in Los Angeles?"

"I believe I've offended you," Towns said.

"I believe you have," said the fellow. Then, in the style of a trial attorney with a witness on the hook, he asked Towns if he had been to such-and-such a place and such-and-such a place, rattling off a dozen winners and not waiting for Towns to say he hadn't heard of this one or hadn't gotten around to that other one. The once-friendly fellow then gave Towns the world's thinnest smile and went to sleep. In Los Angeles, Towns tried a few of the fellow's suggestions and had to admit they were first-rate, although they tended to go in as heavily for ceremony as they did for food. A waitress would come over, curtsy, and say, "I am Mary Jo Smith, your waitress for tonight, and here is your special chilled fork for the Brazília Festival Salad." If anyone had tried that on him in New York, he or one of his friends would have done twenty minutes on it, probably right in front of the offending Mary Jo Smith. And they would have been wrong. Except that you could not admit that you liked elaborate curtsied ceremonies in New York. It seemed perfectly all right in Los Angeles.

More than the restaurants and movie theaters and homes, it was the getting to them that he really enjoyed. He loved getting dressed in the cool shady early evening and then stopping in the middle since all you ever had to be was half-dressed in L. A. It was not very typical of his life, but he had once taken a journey that had brought

5

him to ancient walled-up cities in Central Asia. It was probably the only quick trip anyone had ever taken to that part of the world. He had been scouting a movie location and was in and out in five days. He would not have wanted the job of convincing anyone of this, but that high, dizzy, pulsing sensation he experienced each time he approached the Strip was every bit as profound as what he felt upon first seeing the outlines of Samarkand. Always he was astonished by the cleanness of the light along the Strip, the slow, clean tumble of beautiful blond children, the outrageous brilliance of the high posters advertising Lake Tahoe entertainment trios but looking more like huge films shown in the sky. How did they get those pictures so large and startling and clear . . .

He was aware, of course, that much of it had to do with him and not California. He was fond of saying, "When I get to the West Coast, there's absolutely no hassle." He used such expressions in California. He said sullen people were "downers," an unfortunate experience was "a bad trip," and even caught himself describing a lively woman as a "dynamite chick." He did not talk that way in New York. There was always someone who would make a face. In New York, the pressure was on to come up with new ones. You could get away with a slightly tired expression if you were careful to put it in italics. Or if it was really old, you were safe in bringing it back. Now those were the rules, take it or leave it.

In California, Harry Towns had no debts, no broken marriage, no glum and heartbroken feelings of work undone. Let him pass a day in New York without "accomplishing" something and he would feel his stomach slowly being drawn out of him. In California, there were always going to be other days. There was always plenty of time.

He would feel the drumbeat of excitement the moment he got on the plane and headed for the West Coast. Forty-five minutes on a plane to anyplace else was a lifetime for Harry Towns. But the five-hour run to Los Angeles was a luxury.

He was a stranger in L. A., and he intended to keep it that way. There was no one looking over his shoulder, no one taking notes. He would not arrive in Los Angeles so much as "roll into town" in the style of mysterious Western heroes slowly loping into strange Montana outposts. He preferred keeping relationships (not a favorite word —but they hadn't come up with a better one) casual, transient, and when he got to L. A. there was no one he raced to the phone to call. His one close friend was a chemist who had never gotten married and was arrested, socially, at the college level; he loved to reminisce about beautiful sorority girls they had both known as Lambda Chi's at Purdue. Most were named Jo Ann or Sally Anne or Annie Lou, names in that family. This fellow had been in a mild, almost imperceptible depression from the moment Towns met him—and it was catching—so Harry Towns had dinner with him only once a trip. It was no fun being with someone who was always "a little low."

Harry Towns had a sprinkling of other friends in L. A., a bartender here, a waitress there, some people in the film colony. One in particular would gather a small group of guests and show them spanking new rough cuts of feature-length films after first distributing old-fashioned candy bars that were a foot long. That was fine once in a while. But what Harry Towns loved most to do was set out in the evening with no date and no particular destination, relying on the peculiar sense of recklessness that possessed him in California. In New York, he might be struck by the beauty of a salesgirl, flirt with her a bit, and then settle for a week's worth of tormented dreams. In Los Angeles, if a girl fell into an intriguing posture, more often than not he would simply scoop her up and whisk her away for the night. Or at least take a good shot at it. In most situations, he did not have the faintest idea of what he was going to do. It made him feel dangerous, and this turned him into exciting company for himself. He felt like a loaded gun. In the event his nightly quests for adventure ended up a bit wilted, he had a few fallback positions. The nostalgic chemist was one. There was a slightly over-the-hill TV ingenue who would generally take him in. She was double-jointed and knew erotic postures which she would fall into the moment he opened the door. He also knew one late-night club where he could count on a few familiar faces.

Harry Towns was aware, too, of a special tribe of long-legged golden women who roamed the area, evading him, dancing slightly beyond his reach. Some called them vacant, mindless, not worth the trouble. Dingalings. Subject them to close inspection and you would see the flaws. A dark-haired dancer he knew saw him staring at a pack of them and said, "They're not worthy of you." But how he yearned for them. On previous trips, his adventures had been with cashiers, hustlers, leftover women on the frayed corners of L. A. life. But he had always felt an awareness of that golden tribe, eyes aloof, carriage regal, long hair trickling down delicious tan shoulders. On this trip, it had somewhat come together for him. Early on, he found an angry one. Angry when he met her, angry in bed, skulking off in a furor after a night of angered, begrudging love. She told him that, yellow hair, perfect legs, and all, she had been badly manhandled by an actor with a marred career. Perhaps what really irritated her was that Harry Towns had trapped her, straggling beyond the golden caravan. In any case, she was an official card-carrying member of the tribe. He had made contact. Soon after, he found another, standing high and golden on a stationery store ladder. Dusting boxes. "A girl like you dusting?" he said, not the most spectacular remark. But she went for it. All things were possible in Los Angeles. "Actually," she said, "I've been looking for something with more bite to it." He took her back to the hotel and at one point made her get out of bed and stand on a ladder, stationery-store style. Was he some kind of ladder freak? Even if he was, it was all right with her. Watching her that way, he fought for his breath. He had one of those extraordinary sun girls up on a ladder, tan legs straining, just for him. L. A. was some town.

It had been that kind of trip—fat, rich, lazy, most of the treasures of Beverly Hills one room-service call away. Now, at poolside on a late Friday afternoon, Towns felt the first stirrings of regret at having to leave Los Angeles. His work was completed. If he stayed any longer, he would have to pay his own bills. Not an attractive prospect for Harry Towns. All dollars aside, it struck him that part of the magical fun of Los Angeles was having someone else pay your way. They knew exactly how to pay you, too. The right style. After he had arrived on this trip, he had told his producer he was "a little short." That afternoon, he found twenty one-hundred-dollar bills in his hotel mailbox; they were so crisp and new he could shave with them. For all he knew, he may even have been losing a few thousand on the deal. That didn't seem

important. Having those razor-sharp bills in his pocket—
and getting them so fast—made everything seem fine.

Harry Towns had to visit his son at summer camp
within the next week, so he would be leaving in any case.
He had promised to store up anecdotes about film stars
for the youngster. So far Towns had only run into stars of
Forties movies who weren't going to mean anything to the
boy. He reminded himself to go that night to places where
the stars hung out and try to see some for the boy so he
could report on what they were up to.

The crowning touch to this trip had been a lovely
divorcee who had appeared at the pool the day before. He
did a quick fantasy thumbnail sketch on her—as he
always did on people who interested him. He made her
out to be the wife of a doctor, a marvelous dinner-party
giver, very strong on fund raising for charities; the doctor
was indeed to be congratulated because she kept herself
in marvelous trim, working hard at it since she had to be
getting on in her thirties. A private thing about her was
that she was given to sudden and delightful thrusts of
vulgarity, both in and out of bed. The combination of fund-
raising good looks and the flash of dirty stuff was irresist-
ible. He did some laps in the pool, had a breath-holding
contest with himself to see how much older he was
getting, and when he surfaced, wet, bearded, and shining,
at the shallow end, she was waiting for him, legs tucked
beneath her. "The Christ resemblance really does cry out
for comment," she said. She was a three-time loser in
marriage, had a grown son, and had run away from her
third husband, registering anonymously in the hotel. Her
husband lived about twelve miles away. He was not a

doctor. He owned close-out shoe stores which ran regular disaster sales. But at least Towns was right about the dinner parties. He was not very far off target on the sudden flashes of vulgarity, either. Towns was not sure he would be able to get that favorite California wine of his in New York, and now that he was leaving, he wanted to have as much of it as possible. Over glasses of it, she said she had been in love only once, to a silent boy who drifted in and out of her life at college. After graduation, he dropped her a note from Thailand and that was it. After an incredibly short period, she looked at Towns and said, "I fear it's happening to me a second time." They drifted back to Towns's suite. Why was it so easy to get girls to drift back to suites in California? They made love for a short while; he marked her down as the kind of woman who liked to spend a short time making love and a long time analyzing its ramifications. "It's not been that good for me," she said. "In so many ways I wish I had never noticed a tanned and bearded fellow coming out of the pool like Christ reborn." She said, however, that any time he wanted her, no matter where he was, she would come to him and he could use her in any way he wanted, so long as it didn't involve having another girl watch, or anything in that family. (He had a feeling she could be pushed in that direction, too. Otherwise, why would she have brought it up?) When he was a younger man, such an invitation would have paralyzed his senses. Now it only sounded fairly good. In any case, she left a bracelet behind and then called to ask if she could come by to get it.

So now he waited for her, and it occurred to him that all he had done to attract her was act a bit distant, keeping his jaw set as though he had been through some grim times and didn't want to talk about them. He reminded himself to do that more often instead of shooting for charm. It occurred to him that if his wife were to meet him for the first time now—and he were to behave the way he had with the divorcee—she would be terribly attracted to him and not be in Dubrovnik. But you never knew.

Late in the afternoon, he began to get a little edgy. He wished the girl would come get her bracelet and disappear. There was some good sun remaining and it was almost as if he could not really soak it up properly if he were scanning about looking for someone. He thought about the astronauts and felt guilty about his plan to skip over the flight to the moon and come in at the last minute for the landing. And he was sorry he had not been involved in the historic flight in any way. Editorials were saying that all Americans were involved in the landing, but he was living evidence of one who wasn't. Even doing public-relations work for an outfit that built computers would have been something. Why wasn't he at least stationed opposite a TV set, urging on the astronauts? One thing he had to do was get a great new set for the occasion. The stores would be closed in New York on Sunday, so he would have to pick one up in Los Angeles and take it back with him. It was a way of showing respect to the space program and, he supposed, to the country. Instead of hanging out a flag, he would finally get a clear TV set.

When she showed up, cool and blonde in a white dress, he changed his mind about wanting to get rid of her quite that fast. He was not exactly overbrimming with desire, but on the other hand there was no point in letting her slip away either. In a sense, he supposed he was "using" her and, if such were the case, that had to be unattractive. But wasn't she "using" him, too? Hadn't she made him up? Seen him at the pool and gone right ahead and invented him? Would he be doing her a favor if he said, "Look, I'm not Christ, I'm not that silent drifting fellow who ended up in Thailand, I'm Harry Towns, slightly unhappy at the moment, hanging out, and delighted to fuck an attractive woman whenever I get the opportunity." If he said that to her, or some variation thereof, would it make him a better person? He didn't see it as being all that clear-cut.

They had some more of the great wine and she said, "Just talking to you I feel I'm making love to you."

"I don't feel that way," he said.

"Then why don't you grab me by the neck and take me back to your room?"

"I don't do that," he said.

She went back with him anyway; the thing he noticed was that he was incapable of making any wrong moves with this woman. If he had gone into a furious bout of nose-picking, she would have found something charming about it. Harry Towns's comparisons generally fell into the sports division. So he saw it as one of those days when every junk shot you threw up automatically put two points on the board.

"Have you noticed," she said, during the period given over to analysis, "that in our lovemaking I've been concerned primarily with pleasing you and not the slightest in pleasing myself?"

"I wondered about that," he said. After she left, he checked to make sure she hadn't left any more bracelets around.

He was happy she was gone, but as soon as he was

alone in the room, he decided it was not going to go well if he hung around any longer; he might as well leave Los Angeles as soon as possible, more or less on a high note. He boosted his spirits by telling himself that California was fine, but you got flabby there. Inside and outside. New York was mean, cruel, nerve-wracking—but it was only in such an atmosphere that you stayed prepared to do battle. He believed that, incidentally. And he had not yet reached the stage in life where he was ready to "take it easy." He might never.

Early the next morning, he bought a small TV set from a tiny Japanese man who said it was a new model and he was very proud of it. Towns couldn't get over how sharp and clear the picture was. He was not mechanically in-clined—and didn't particularly want to be. Probably for that reason he loved tiny, intricately made gadgets; he had a vision of filling up a warm, comfortable apartment with them, living in it, and spending most of his time turning them on and off. You couldn't do that to people, but you could do it to gadgets. And they didn't go wrong, the way people did. If a gadget malfunctioned, you threw it away and got another one. He was probably feeling a little let down about people at the moment. Ironically, a sudden burst of love came over him for the tiny Japanese man who was practically a transistor himself. He wanted to bend over and give him a hug. Why couldn't he just do that? The fellow was so tiny that Towns had to wonder what would happen if the man caught a disease that made him lose weight. He would probably just get a little smaller and become healthy again. The fellow fixed up the TV package with a tricky little tissue-paper handle so that Towns wouldn't chafe his hands carrying it. He loved the handle almost as much as he did the TV set. The

American version of that handle would have involved rows of factory workers and probably would not have been as comfortable to the hand. Admittedly, it would have lasted longer. In any case, he promised himself that he would go to Japan some day, although he was convinced he would be guilty of hair-raising breaches of etiquette the instant he set foot in the country.

He didn't want to hang around any longer. As soon as he got back to his hotel, he changed his plane reservation so that he would be back in New York in plenty of time to watch the moon landing on the delicious little new TV set. Then he had a last lunch in Los Angeles in a marvelously crumbled outdoor restaurant, ordering a final bottle of the great wine. It never occurred to him that he could get the same wine in New York. It wouldn't taste the same anyway. Though he had no authorities to back him up, he was convinced that California wines didn't travel well. The driver who took him to the airport said Towns looked like he was in the film business and asked if Towns could get him a copy of a film script, any script at all, so that he could study the form and then try one of his own. Towns couldn't see why they were so hard to get—surely libraries and bookstores carried tons of them—but the fellow said you would be surprised how tough it was to get one. He seemed desperate, so Towns took his address and said when he got to New York he would certainly try to rustle one up. It was the kind of assignment he would take a long time getting around to, although it would always be slightly on his mind. Maybe he would follow through and maybe he wouldn't. He had dozens of those.

His idea was to take the little TV set back to his apartment in New York City and watch the moon landing

there. The timing was set up just right. All that had to
happen was for the plane to land on schedule and not get
involved in any traffic tie-ups over JFK. One of the stewardesses sat next to Towns in the lounge and told him she
had been closed up for a long time, all through her child-
hood, but that she had opened up the previous fall. If
Towns had been going to Los Angeles and not coming
back from it, he probably would have asked if she was
open or closed at the moment, but as it was, he let it slide.
He didn't like to start in when he was on his way to New
York. As it happened, the plane landed on time, but the
porter who picked up his luggage slammed the TV box
onto his luggage carrier and then heaved a massive suitcase on top of it; Towns was sure he had done some
critical damage to the set. "Don't you know there's a
goddamn little TV set in there," he said to the porter. In
some strange way, he took it all as a direct attack on the
tiny polite Japanese man. "I didn't know that," said the
porter. "Anyway, there's no way to guarantee smooth
passage."

He had the feeling that no little TV set could survive a
shot like that so he took it out of the box, attached the
battery pack and switched it on at the terminal. Some
sputtering pictures showed up. "See that," said the porter,
"she coming in good." It came as no great surprise to
Towns when the pictures bleeped out and turned to dark-
ness. There was a package of warranties in the box, but
Towns had no heart to get involved with them. Besides,
he had the feeling that once a mechanical gadget was
injured, it went downhill no matter what you did to it. He
gave the porter a look and then tossed the set lightly into
a trash container. That style—casually throwing away

something of value—was a bit of a carry-over from Los Angeles. Someone in the terminal said the astronauts were going to be down in forty-five minutes. There wasn't any time to fool around now. Towns kept a key to his wife's house on the outskirts of the city and told a cabbie to take him there. She had not asked to have the key back, and he hadn't handed it over to her either. The cabbie was certain Towns was going to get in the cab and then say he really wanted to go to Brooklyn. All through the ride he kept looking around suspiciously at Towns, expecting to be told to swerve off the highway and head back to the hated faraway borough. When they were well out in the suburbs, the cabbie relaxed and said he couldn't believe his luck, getting a call to go to the country and not Brooklyn. As they neared the house, Towns became a little apprehensive even though he knew his wife was in Yugoslavia and his son was off to camp. Maybe he would find something he didn't like in there, a boyfriend, for example, sleeping in his old bed.

The house was a little damp, but otherwise it was eerily the way he had left it, with no signs of orgiastic frenzy. A next door neighbor's house was occupied and Towns wondered if his kid was being teased for not having a dad around. If his own father had ever stepped out of the picture—to the extent that Towns had—he was sure he would not have been able to handle it. No father around! He would have run his head into something. Taken himself out that way. So how could his own kid possibly handle it? Maybe he was a stronger kid than Towns had been. Or was he running his head into the wall in some way Towns didn't know about? Then again, Harry Towns tried to stay in there—nice and tight—even when he was traveling—at least as far as the boy was concerned. So that had to make a difference. These notions never once occurred to him in Los Angeles.

He stayed in the kitchen awhile, eating a slice of Swiss cheese that seemed to be in remarkably good shape. The kitchen was the most beautiful room in the house, jammed with extraordinary knickknacks that had been accumulated over the years of the marriage. He felt a little sorry for himself, spending all that time and money helping to accumulate knickknacks and then never again getting to enjoy them. He had often said that possessions didn't mean a thing; all that counted were friendships and how you felt, but he sure did love knickknacks and wondered if he shouldn't have taken a few along. He had scooped up some of his slacks and jackets and a handful of terrific books, but not one knickknack. And it didn't seem fair to swipe a few with his wife away. He went upstairs then, still with a shade of expectation that he would find a guy up there, sleeping in his old bed and waiting for his old wife to get back from Dubrovnik. What if his wife took up with a fellow who was a strict disciplinarian and went around disciplining his kid? Towns would have to come back and slam the guy around a little. He might have to kill him.

He decided to watch the landing in his son's room. That way, when he went up to visit the boy, he would be able to give him a report on how his room was getting along. The boy had a TV set propped up next to his bed and Towns remembered bawling out the kid when he saw him smack the set a few times to get it into focus. It turned out that the boy was right and the only way to get it to work properly was to smack it around a few times. The boy's room was filled with drawings that featured cartoon apes leaping from the tops of skyscrapers. The boy had some talent as an artist and Towns figured the leaping apes just represented a period he was going through, although he had to admit he had certainly been in that period for a long time. He wasn't too worried about it. All men who had amounted to anything had probably done things that seemed a little weird at the time. He checked around the room, getting the feel of the kid again and remembering some of the time he had spent in there, helping him fix it up. Then he sat down on the boy's bed and spotted the empty animal cage. The previous year, with the boy away at camp, he had gotten a call from the camp director saying the boy missed his pet mouse and maybe Towns ought to bring it up to camp on visiting day. As far as the director was concerned it would put the summer over the top for the kid. Towns was feeling low about the marriage, which was splitting up at the time, and would have brought up an elephant if he had been asked. So he set out in his car and drove to Vermont with the white mouse in the back, throwing him a carrot whenever the animal got a little restless. That night he stopped off in New Hampshire at a motel, with the idea that he would head for camp early the next morning. The motel had a sign that said no pets. He registered anyway, and slipped the animal cage into the room when the owner wasn't looking. He had dinner at a local cabaret that featured a Middle-Eastern dancer who let you put your hand in her panties if you stuck dollars in there, too. Towns didn't see himself going that way, but when his turn came he shoved in two singles. When he got back to the motel, he caught the owner in his car headlights, standing with his legs spread apart and pointing to the grass. When Towns got out of the car, the owner said, "I told you no pets." The animal was lying on its back in the grass, cold and frozen, a sightless eye fixed at the moon. Towns marked the motel owner's face for life with a heavy ring he wore on his finger and for all he knew he had purchased for just such an occasion. He had to use lawyers, but he got away with it. He thought about it for months afterward and still did; he felt that if he had another go-round at the same situation, he would handle it exactly the same way, not varying one beat. At camp, he told the boy the animal had caught cold and died peacefully and painlessly in an animal hospital. He said he would get the boy any pet in the world, but the boy said he didn't want any more and kept the empty cage in his room with the door open.

Towns wondered if the astronauts went through things like that, whether they had ugly split-ups with wives who subsequently ran off to Dubrovnik, boys who drew pictures of apes leaping from buildings, if they ever wound up scarring men in far-off roadside motels at midnight. His first impulse was to feel no, they didn't. They were too sober and well-rooted for that kind of nonsense. Weren't they from "the other America," as it was so commonly felt in those circles that were contemptuous of chilled forks and Brazília Festival salads? Where were the Puerto Rican astronauts? Where were the black ones? He couldn't recall seeing any spacemen of the Hebraic persuasion running around either. But then again, Towns remembered pictures of the pinched and weary faces of some of the astronauts' wives and it became his guess that all wasn't as tidy as it came off in the national magazines. He knew what those long separations for work did to marriages. There was probably no beating the system even if you were a non-ethnic space pioneer and your wife was an astronautical winner. He decided they were men, too, some good, some not so hot. They had experienced failure, ate too much marinara sauce on occasion, vomited appropriately, lusted after models, worried about being a fag, about having cancer, even had an over-quick ejaculation or two. These thoughts comforted Harry Towns somewhat as he sat down on his boy's bed, gave the TV set a few shots to get it started, and prepared to watch the fulfillment of man's most ancient dream.

②
THE
Partners

impending divorce might suddenly show up in his face as a rash. Towns would say, "Sure, how about you?" The boy would answer, "Fine." They kept reassuring themselves in that way but holding onto each other all the same. Towns did not really know the boy very well. He had taken him for granted, as he might have a fine, reliable watch that would inevitably be right there on his wrist whenever he wanted it. Now that it looked as though the family would break up officially, he had moved forward in a clumsy rush to spend more time with the boy, some of it play-acting, some of it an honest attempt to savor the child and store up moments with him as though building a secret bank account. He had asked the boy where he would like to go for a trip and the boy had picked Las Vegas, aware of the gambling, but probably mixing it up a little with Los Angeles although he would never admit this to his father. Towns could have straightened him out on this, but he didn't, figuring he could sneak in a little gambling himself, and at the same time, see to it that the boy had a terrific time. There were some slot machines in the terminal, but a sign said you couldn't play them unless you were twenty-one or over. The boy was disappointed and wondered whether he could slip a few coins in anyway when no one was looking. His father said all right, that he would act as a lookout, but after the boy had played three quarters, Towns got nervous about it and stopped him. "I think they mean it," he said. "I think they can lose their license."

"That's too bad," said the boy. "Because I know those are lucky ones. I can tell those are the best in Las Vegas."

"It's too risky," said Towns. "Right at the airport. Maybe when we get deeper in."

The reservation story had been dismal, but a friend of

Towns had gotten them fixed up in a small, little-known hotel on the edge of town, saying that a famous bandleader always stayed there when the Sands was overbooked. It was called The Regent; they took a cab to it and found it to be a noisy, rugged little place, one with a half-dozen slots and two blackjack tables in the lobby. An Indian with coveralls and a great perspired shine on his face was the only blackjack player. "That fellow's an Indian," Towns whispered to the boy as they approached the desk. "So what," said the boy. He was always quick to spot it whenever Towns passed on formally educational little bits.

The room was quite small and Towns was embarrassed about the size of it, feeling that he had let the boy down. But the boy said he loved it; he got into his pajamas and leapt into bed with miracle speed. "It's my favorite hotel in the world," he said.

"We're going to have a great time," said Towns, tucking in the boy and clearing back his hair so that he could kiss his forehead. "I'll kill myself to see to it."

"You don't have to kill yourself," said the boy.

Towns turned out the lights and then went into the bathroom to treat his crabs. He had gotten a case of them a week before he had left for Las Vegas and felt terribly degraded about it, mostly because his new girlfriend was from Bryn Mawr and there was a chance he had passed them along to her just before he had left. There was also a distant possibility he had gotten them from her, but he didn't want to think about that. The thing he hated most was the name: crabs. The medicine bottle referred to them as body lice and that was a little better but still didn't do the trick. The doctor said that if he shampooed his body, they would go away in nine out of ten cases, but

27

he couldn't imagine that happening. "Once you have them on the run," an adventurous friend had told Harry Towns, "they can be amusing." Maybe that was true if you were bogged down in trench warfare at the Marne, but to Harry Towns they didn't have a single delightful aspect. He just wanted to see them on their way. He soaped himself up with the medicine, stood around for ten minutes, in accordance with the directions, and then hopped into the shower and soaped himself some more. He got the feeling somehow that he was spreading them to other parts of his body, the hair on top of his head, for example. When he got out of the shower, the boy, hollering through the door, asked him why he was taking so long. "I'm just relaxing in here," he said.

The doctor had told him to get rid of all clothing that had come into contact with the crabs and he did that, throwing away his underwear. He was reminded of a fellow at college who threw away suits of underwear after a single day's wear. And that was without crabs. At the time, Towns couldn't imagine anyone rich enough to toss away underwear after one use; years later, he came to the conclusion that the fellow was unhappy and was trying to catch his unloving parents' attention. Meanwhile, Towns had to figure out how to deal with his suit. He decided to hang onto it and keep his fingers crossed that a stray crab hadn't wandered onto the fabric. He carefully hid the medicine bottle so that the boy wouldn't accidentally come across it and ask what it was. Then he got into a pair of fresh pajamas and slid into bed; the boy was sleeping, and it seemed to Towns that he itched more than ever and that he had roused the crabs to a fury, and sent them scurrying far and wide. He went into the bathroom and, not knowing whether he was awake or dreaming, began to shave off his pubic hair, being very cautious and tentative at first and then warming to the task and slashing it off with great verve. He took some off his stomach, too, and began his chest but then stopped and said the hell with it. He looked at himself in the mirror, standing on a chair so that he could see the shaved areas, and decided he looked very new and young and unusual. It was a little exciting. But then he realized there was no way to get the hair back on; indeed, he had no idea how quickly it would grow back or if it would grow back at all. It still itched like hell, but he knew it couldn't have been the crabs that were doing it and this was comforting. In bed, he realized that he would have to tell his Bryn Mawr girl he had them and wondered how she would react to that. It made him sick to think about it. He decided to tell her he had "body lice" but then changed his mind and went over to straight "crabs." He would simply hit her with it—"I've got the crabs"—and if she ran away, he would get along without her, even though she was quite gentle and extraordinary. He would then have to find a girl who had these qualities and was also tough-minded enough to accept crabs.

In the morning, the boy was dressed and ready to roll by the time Towns opened his eyes. The itching had kept him awake most of the night, leaving him tired and irritable. It seemed to Towns that getting out of bed and being easy and kind to the boy was going to be the single hardest thing he had ever done in his life. He felt inside his pajamas on the slim chance that he had only dreamed about the shaving, but he was clean as a whistle. "Do you think we can play the slots before breakfast or shall we wait till afterward?" asked the boy. When Towns reminded him that you had to be twenty-one to play them, the boy fell back in astonishment and slapped his head, saying "What?" as though Towns were giving him the information for the first time. All through their trip, the boy was to pretend it was all right for him to play the slots and fall back in amazement when Towns reminded him that he couldn't. Towns didn't know whether to be irritated or pleased by this stunt and decided finally that it was a good thing for the boy to keep trying in the face of ridiculous odds. On the way downstairs, Towns told the boy he was going to be scratching himself a lot on the trip. "That's because I've picked up a skin condition," he told the boy. "It can drive you nuts."

"I hope it clears up, Dad," said the boy.

As soon as they hit the street, Towns realized there wasn't going to be much you could do with a young boy in Las Vegas. Gambling was the name of the game; Los Angeles, of course, with Disneyland, would have been the correct choice. To compensate for this, Towns made a big fuss over every little thing they did. When their breakfast eggs were served to them at a small diner, Towns said, "Well, there they are, Las Vegas eggs." The boy went along with Towns, saying, "Las Vegas eggs, that's great." But when they went out to the main street and Towns said, "Look at this place, isn't it something?" the boy said, "I don't see what's so wonderful about it. Maybe it is, but it's hard to tell so far." Towns wondered if they ought to rent a car and drive to Los Angeles after all; but then he decided that the important thing was that they be together and draw very close. He put his arm around the boy's shoulders and the boy, pretending they were the same height, reached way up and got his arm around his father's shoulder. They walked lopsidedly through the main street of Las Vegas that way. The boy was something of a coin collector and when they got to a shop that sold them, Towns took twenty dollars of the money he had more or less set aside for gambling and gave it to the boy so he could buy some special ones.

"I don't know whether I should be taking this away from you, Dad," said the boy.

"It's all right," said Towns. "I want to give it to you."

"But I feel it will hurt you if I take it," said the boy, looking very sad and sick.

"You'll be making me happy," said Towns. "My own folks made me feel guilty when they gave me things and I don't want that to happen to you." Hearing his own words, it seemed to Towns that he was trying to be a wonderful parent in a big hurry, leaping at every opportunity to get across slices of wisdom. So he promised himself he would try to be a little more natural. Towns waited for the boy outside the coin shop, feeling restless about being that close to all the gambling and not having gotten to it quite yet. It would be obscene to make a trip to Las Vegas and not get in any gambling, but he knew he had to feed the boy a certain number of good times before he thought about the tables. The boy came out after a bit and said, "Let's get out of here, Dad. I think I just got a coin that's worth thousands and the man hasn't caught on to it yet. Is there any way he can trace us back to our hotel?"

Towns told the boy he was kidding himself and that it was a lot harder than that to make money in life. "That man's been in the coin business for a long time," said Towns. "He knows more about it than you and doesn't give away thousands that easily." More wisdom. The boy said he was sure the coin was worth a fortune, but he said it with little conviction and Towns felt like digging a ditch for himself. Why couldn't he just go along with the kid and let him dream? "Maybe you're right," he said. "Hell, I don't know much about coins." But he said it much too late for it to do any good.

That afternoon, Towns, desperate for young-boy activities, signed up for a bus visit to a dam that bridged two states, Nevada and Arizona. When the boy found out they were going to a dam, he said, "I'm not sure I'd love to do that," and Towns, short with him for the first time, said, "Cut it out. We're going. You don't come all the way out here and not go to their dam." On the bus, the itching got the best of him and he was sure he had come up with a type of crab that actually ducked down beneath the skin and couldn't be shaved off. He felt sorry for himself, an about-to-be-divorced guy, riding out to a dam with crabs and a young boy. At the dam site, the guide lectured the group about hardships involved in the building of the dam and Towns said to the boy, "They must have had some job. Imagine, coming out here, starting with nothing and having to put up a dam."

The boy said, "Dad, I'm not enjoying this. I just came out here because you wanted to. I don't want to hurt your feelings, but I'm not having that great a time."

"You can't always have a great time," said Towns. "Not every second of your life."

When the guide led the tour group through the bottom of the dam and into Arizona, the boy perked up considerably. "That's great," said the boy, running around in the small area. "I'm in Arizona. It's great here and that means I've been to another state." He kept careful track of all the states he'd been to and even counted ones he had just nicked the edges of on car rides.

That night, Towns told the boy to dress up and he would take him to one of the big shows at a hotel on the Strip. He found out the name of one that admitted kids and when they got to it, he gave the headwaiter a huge tip to make sure they were put at a fine table. The head-waiter led them into the dining room, through a labyrinth of tables, getting closer and closer to the stage, the boy turning back to his father several times to say, "Look how close we're getting. How come he's taking us to such a great table?" The headwaiter put them at ringside right up against the stage, and the boy said, "This is fabulous. He must think we're famous or something." Towns smiled and said, "He must." He didn't mention anything about the tip, but after they had eaten shrimp cocktails, he told the boy he had given the headwaiter some money, tram-pling on the dream again. "Oh," said the boy, a little forlorn. There was just nothing Towns could do to con-trol himself. On the other hand, maybe it was wise to fill the boy in on tipping behavior. Otherwise, he might won-der, later on, why he wasn't getting fabulous tables on his own hook. Towns had been to Las Vegas several years back and he remembered the women being a lot prettier. "The girls look a little hard, don't they?" he said to the boy, realizing he was trying to draw his son out on his feelings about women. "They're okay," said the boy, who didn't seem to want to dig into the subject.

The show was a huge, awkward one with plenty of raz-zle-dazzle. When it was over, the boy said it was the great-est show he had ever seen and wondered why they didn't bring a show like that to New York. "They might," said Towns, "and you'd be able to say you'd seen it first out here." The casino was bulging with activity, Towns feel-ing the lure and magnetism of it. "I wouldn't mind doing a little gambling," he said to the boy and saw that he was asking his permission. He did that often and wondered if it was proper behavior. Once, they had gone "mountain climbing" on a giant slag heap in their town. The boy was great at it, shooting right to the top, but Towns looked back over his shoulder, got panicky, and the boy had to reach back and grab him. Were you allowed to have your son take over, even momentarily, and become your dad? Towns decided that you were, much later on, but he was getting into it a bit early.

"What if you gambled and lost your money?" the boy asked.

"It doesn't make any difference," said Towns. "You just play for pleasure and never gamble more than you can afford. That way you don't feel bad if you lose." Towns was actually the kind of gambler who fell into deep depressions when he lost a quarter and even got depressed when he won. It wasn't that wonderful for him when he broke even either. Once and for all, he had to stop telling the boy things that seemed nice but that he really didn't believe.

"I couldn't stand it if I lost anything," said the boy. "Therefore I don't think you should gamble."

Towns asked him if he thought he could keep busy for a while and the boy said, "Sure, Dad," with great cheerfulness, but then he asked Towns exactly how long he would be.

"About an hour," said Towns.

"That long, eh?" said the boy.

He went off to roam around the lobby and Towns sat down to play blackjack with a dealer named Bunny. The dealer was slow, and Towns liked that, but he was aware of having to keep an eye on the boy and felt as though only half of him was sitting at the table. The boy would disappear and then bob up between a couple of slots or behind a plant, a duck in a shooting gallery. Towns was edgy as he made his bets, as though some tea was boiling and any second he would have to run out and turn off the gas. He told himself it didn't matter, all that counted was whether the cards came or not, but he didn't believe that for a second. He felt that the boy, running around the lobby, had a strong effect on the cards he was drawing. A dark-haired, hard-looking woman played at the seat on his right; she was attractive, although Towns felt she was just a fraction over the line and into hooker territory. He wondered whether it would be possible to dash up to a room with her and still nip back to the tables before the hour was up. That arrangement would be just fine for a Las Vegas hooker. Then he remembered the shaving and knew it wouldn't work out. Hooker or not, she would be experienced enough to know something wasn't exactly right. Towns forgot whether he was winning or losing. The boy called him away from the tables at one point and said, "Dad, I don't want to disturb your game, but a man wants to kill me." Towns knew that the boy had a way of dramatizing routine events, but he followed him nevertheless to a Spanish busboy who leaned against the wall of the dining room and didn't back up for a second when he saw Towns coming. "You bothering the kid?" said Towns, standing very close to the man. "That's right," said the busboy, "he spoiling the rhythm of the place."

"Just lay off him," said Towns, pushing a finger up against the man's face. He had planned to do just that no matter what the man said.

"Tell him to behave then," said the busboy, not backing up an inch.

"I'll take care of him and you lay off him," said Towns, breaking away from the man, as though in victory.

"Do you think you could have taken him?" asked the boy as they walked back to the casino.

"I don't know," said Towns. "I wasn't thinking about that."

"I've never seen you really fight a guy," said the boy. "I think I'd like that."

"I've had some fights," said Towns. "The trick is to get what you want without fighting. Any animal can fight. Any time you do, you automatically lose."

"I think I'd like to see you do it once," said the boy, and Towns realized that once again he was saying things to the boy that he hated. If someone had given him the kind of advice he was passing along to the child, he would have vomited. He was feeding him stuff he felt he was expected to feed him. But who expected it?

"Are you going to gamble some more?" asked the boy. "Your hour's up."

"It's a little hard when you have someone along," said Towns.

"Do you understand why they don't let children gamble?" the boy asked. Towns started to tell him it led to other things like missing school and crime, but then he said, "Strike that. It's garbage. I don't know why they don't let kids gamble. It would probably be all right." Towns felt proud of his honesty, but the boy didn't seem to care for it much and said, "I thought you knew the answer to things like that."

It suddenly occurred to Towns that it might be a good idea for them to spend their two remaining days at the giant plush Strip hotel. On a hunch, he asked the clerk whether there were rooms available and the clerk said yes, there had been a few checkouts. Towns and the boy made a dash back to their small hotel in town where they packed quickly, the boy saying, "I don't know about this. I liked it here. And I don't want to hurt this hotel's feelings."

"You can't hurt a hotel's feelings," Towns told him. They checked into an enormous, heavily gadgeted room in the Strip hotel and the boy said, "I admit this is great, but the other one was great, too."

The hotel was bigger and cleaner and noisier than the other one, but when you took a careful look at it there wasn't that much more for boys to do at it. Towns checked on some saddle horses the next day, but nobody knew where the stable was or how to get to it. He heard about a college nearby and made a feeble attempt to sell it to the boy, saying, "Imagine, a Las Vegas college. I wonder what it would be like," but the boy didn't even nibble at that one. Towns knew that the swimming pool was closed, but he led the boy out to it anyway; they took off their shirts and sat in chairs alongside the empty concrete pool.

"Is this what you want to do?" asked the boy.

"Just for a while."

"What good's a suntan?"

"They're great," said Towns. "You've forgotten that it's cold back East. It's good to take advantage of things like this."

"I'll get one if you say so, Dad," said the boy. "I don't really want one, but I'll get one."

They ate dinner at a Chinese restaurant that night. On the way to it, Towns took a wistful look at the casino and his son did, too. "Maybe I can play the slots at this one," said the boy.

"You won't quit, will you?"

"I thought maybe since this was a big hotel on the Strip they let boys play."

"They don't," said Towns. He thought of a tough friend of his who had four little girls and almost died because he didn't have a son; he had the feeling that somehow his friend would see to it, if he had a son, that the boy got to play the slots. And Towns wasn't able to pull it off. At the Chinese restaurant, Towns told the boy he loved Chinese food so much that he often thought he could eat it every night of the week. The boy took hold of that, saying, "*Every* night? For the rest of your life?"

"That's right," said Towns. "I think I've had enough at the end of each meal, but the next day I'm ready to have some more."

"That's amazing," said the boy, who was thoroughly pleased by the thought. "I never knew that about you."

The Chinese restaurant had a girl singer who did old Jerome Kern tunes. After she went offstage, Towns, who knew his boy had a singing voice, said to him, "Why don't you get up there and sing a few songs?"

"Are you kidding," said the boy. "Are you crazy? Are you out of your mind? I'd rather be shot dead than get up there."

"You're a singer, aren't you?" said Towns.

"I sing," said the boy, "but are you kidding? You must be crazy, Dad."

Towns said he had a mother who pulled that kind of stuff on him—so he was pulling a little on his son. Only his mother really meant it, whereas Harry Towns was just goofing. The boy loved hearing things about the way it had been for Towns when *he* was young.

On the way back to their hotel, Towns spotted a bowling alley and he suggested they try a few games. It was midnight and he wanted to get at the gambling, but he thought it was the right thing to do and he was proud of himself for the way he was putting himself out for the child.

"I'll bowl with you," said the boy, "but only if you promise it's what you really want to do."

"I promise," said Towns.

The alley was a giant one, completely deserted, and Towns asked the proprietor if anybody ever bowled in Las Vegas. "Not too many," said the proprietor. While they were selecting their balls, the boy said, "How come you just walk up to people and ask them questions?" and Towns answered, "It's a style of mine. I like to find out things. So I figure that's the best way." "I could never do that," said the boy. "That'll change," Towns assured him.

The boy tried several of the balls for size, and after a while declared that there was no ball just right for him in the entire alley and that he probably wouldn't be able to do any great bowling. Towns did not know how to keep score and neither did the boy, so he asked the proprietor to help them out; but even after the old man explained it with great care he still didn't know how to keep score. It was one of those things he knew he would never learn as long as he lived. So he kept a sort of rough score. Towns went over a hundred, by rough count, in the first game, topping the boy, who was amazed and said, "You never told me you were a great bowler. Incredible. And you probably haven't bowled in years either. If you kept it up, you could win thousands of prizes." Towns didn't want to win any prizes. All he wanted to do was get back to the casino and take a try at the tables. He planned to take it easy and let the boy beat him in the second game, but when they got into it, he abandoned his plan and tried as hard as he could and wound up beating the kid again. He always did that with the boy, even in checkers. He just wasn't easygoing enough to let the boy win a few. He told himself it was all right, because when the boy really beat him legitimately, it would mean something. But that was bullshit. It would be better to take it easy once in a while. Of course, it was no picnic finding just the right level— when you had a son. Towns had a feeling he was working too hard at it.

"I'll never be able to beat you as long as I live," said the boy. "Yes, you will," said Towns. "One day you'll go past me and you'll stay ahead forever. All I ask, is that when I become a bent-over old man you won't come along and kick me in the head." He meant it as a joke, but the boy didn't see it that way and said, "Are you kidding, Dad? When I'm older I'll give you every cent I have."

"Just be a good kid," said Towns, "and that's all I'll ever ask."

After the third game, the boy seemed to be settling in for an all-night session. Towns took him by the shoulders and said, "Son, I really would like to do some gambling." The boy took it very well, saying, "Why didn't you say so, Dad? I thought you loved it here."

"I did," said Towns, "but I think I've had my fill."

They returned to the hotel and when the boy was undressed, he said, "What do I do if someone smashes down the door and gets me?"

"Someone won't," said Towns.

"What if you lose?" asked the boy, with real terror in his eyes. It was as though his father was going off to war.

"Then I lose," said Towns. "Meanwhile I've had a lot of fun."

He closed the door and even though he knew it was a sure sign he was going to lose he actually found himself trotting down the hall to the casino. He looked for the slow dealer named Bunny and when he found him, he sat down at the table, got some chips, and, with all the exhilaration of a new thief with his hands on some jewelry, began to gamble. Bunny gave him plenty of time to think and he began to win and at the same time to dispense advice to a fellow next to him who wasn't doing that well.

"Blackjack is the only game where you've got a break. The casino gets its edge from people who really don't know the game, women, for example, who just throw their money away and will split pictures every time they get them."

"Fine," said the man next to him.

Towns played for about three hours, winning four hundred dollars and then stopping, with the idea that he would return on the following night, his last one, and try to bump his winnings into some significant money. He had pulled that off once, in Europe, probably the only time he could think of when he had had no pressing need for the money. He won at roulette, not knowing much about the game, and with no particular system. He won thousands of dollars, a lifetime of luck seemingly crowded into those few weeks of playing in French casinos. He bought a German car-boat with the money, one you could drive up to the edge of the water and then drive in and have it become a boat so that you were driving through the water. And then he sold it. There just weren't enough places where you could drive off a highway and into the water. You had to be living in Canada somewhere, not around New York City.

Before Towns left the table, he told the man next to him that the trick in gambling is to get some of the casino's money and play on that. The man seemed relieved to see him go. Towns cashed in his winnings and when he got back to the hotel he woke the boy at four in the morning. It was one of those things he knew was wrong to do, but he couldn't resist it.

"How'd you do?" asked the boy.

"Won four hundred," said Towns. "And fifty of it is yours, for coins."

"That's not fair," said the boy. "It's your winnings."

"I want to do it for you," said Towns. "You were my partner."

"What if you'd lost?"

"That's different," said Towns.

"I'll take it," said the boy, "but I don't think it's right. I didn't do anything."

"You're my son," said Towns.

They slept late their last full day in Las Vegas and when they awakened in the early afternoon, Towns felt compelled to tell the boy a little about what had happened between the boy's father and mother. "Sometimes people get married young and maybe they shouldn't have and then all of a sudden they're not getting along at all." Of course that wasn't telling him much. He wanted to tell the boy about the Bryn Mawr girl, but if he knew anything he knew that was the wrong thing to do although he was certain the boy would like her. If not on the first meeting, then on the second for sure.

"I'd want to stay with you," said the boy.

"No, you wouldn't," said Towns, but he was pleased the boy had said that. How could he not be?

Towns discovered a gym in the hotel, and after lunch they went into it for a workout. When the boy had stripped down and gone into the workout room, the owner said, "That's terrific the way the kid comes in here. When he grows up he'll have a helluva build on him because he's starting now." Because of the crab situation, Towns was careful to keep himself wrapped in a towel. The gym had some unfamiliar apparatus and he was scared out of his wits that the boy would get tangled up in it and kill himself, or at best hurt his trick knees. All he wanted was for them to work out and get the hell out of there, safe and sound. He hardly did any exercise and spent most of his time warning the boy about the apparatus. A massive black fighter skipped rope in the middle of the floor; Towns recognizing him immediately as a main-eventer who had suffered an important reversal in recent months. Towns moved protectively toward his son, and when the fighter left, he told the child he had been working out right next to a famous fighter. "Why didn't you say so?" said the boy. "I would have asked him what happened in that last fight." Everyone in the gym got a kick out of that, and the owner said, "That's all you would have needed." Towns went in to take a shower, and after a moment, heard a loud noise and then some unnatural stillness. Without looking, he knew what had happened. He walked into the gym and saw his son's body stretched out with a heavy weight over his face. The owner and the masseur were kneeling beside him, the owner saying, "See what happens," and the masseur adding, "Don't move him, you never move them." Towns took his time walking over to the boy, aware that it would look good if he came off as a calm, clear-thinking father. He picked the plate off the boy's face, expecting to see only half a head under there. The boy's eyes were closed and his right cheekbone had an unnatural color, but there was no blood. The boy opened his eyes and asked, "Am I all right? I can't tell. I think I was unconscious for a while, my first time." Towns said he had probably overloaded one side of a barbell with the result that the heavy side tipped over on his head. "It happens to every fellow in a gym," said Towns, "except that the weight doesn't always hit them the way it did you. It'll probably never happen to you again." The boy was delighted that he had been unconscious. "In all my years that never happened to me," he told the owner. The owner said the boy had just been shaken up and that he would be fine, but Towns wasn't so sure and figured the owner was making light of it to fend off a possible lawsuit. He asked for the name of a doctor and when the owner gave him one he called the fellow who said, "Listen, I'm eating dinner thirty miles away." Towns said it was an emergency and the doctor asked, "Were any bones driven into the skull?" When Towns told him he couldn't tell, the doctor said he would meet them in the hotel room. Towns carried the boy up to the room, feeling terrible about what had happened; here he'd watched his son like a hawk and then just two seconds after he'd turned away the boy wound up with weights on his head. Why was he taking his boy to gyms and casinos? Didn't other fathers take their sons camping and duck-hunting? Next thing you knew they'd be passing hookers back and forth. Wait till a judge got wind of the way Towns was bringing up the kid. They'd let him see his son once a year, if he was lucky. "I'm dizzy," said the boy, as Towns put him on the bed, "but I think I'll be all right, except that maybe I won't be." When the doctor arrived, he looked at the boy and said, "The bone hasn't been driven into the skull. He'll be okay, except for the banged-up place." It was a terrible thing to think, but Towns felt guilty about the injury not being a little more serious—to justify taking the doctor away from his dinner on a thirty-mile trip. "I'm positive I'm going into a coma," said the boy. The doctor laughed and when Towns tried to pay him, he put up the palm of his hand in a negative gesture and said, "That's all right, I've got a boy." When the doctor left, the boy said, "I'm sorry to be spoiling your good time," to which Towns replied, "Are you kidding? I'm just thrilled you're all right." Towns packed his face down with ice and sat with the boy while he dozed on and off. If the bone had indeed been tucked back in the boy's skull it would have entailed staying in Las Vegas for days, maybe weeks, or possibly some special kind of plane to get him back East; he was relieved they weren't going to get into that. The boy was good-looking, but in a curious, unconventional way; Towns decided the banged-up cheekbone wasn't going to hold him back much. It would be just another curious feature adding to his curious good looks. The boy said he was a little dizzy and had no appetite so Towns simply sat with him until long after the dinner hour. They were leaving the next morning and Towns wondered if he could get in one last session at the tables and try to boost his winnings to an important level, like that time in France. Only this go-round, he wouldn't buy a German car-boat. He would salt it away, about half for his son. Towns would hand it over to him when he was twenty-one and say, "Here you are, kid, five grand—do anything you like with it." And that would include gambling and hookers, if the boy wanted to go that way. The important thing was not to put any strings on it. When it was close to midnight, he suggested to the kid that he might like to take one last shot at the tables. Appearing to be startled, the boy said, "You would do that? Don't do it, Dad. I was unconscious for a while, the first time in my life." Towns said okay, okay, he wouldn't leave him, and the boy dozed off again. When he awakened, a fraction after midnight, Towns brought it up again. "And don't forget, you're my partner," he said. "If I win, I'll give you a lot of it for coins."

"Okay," said the boy, "but you've got to use some of my money." He sat up a little, reached into his wallet, and took out twenty-five dollars of the fifty his father had given him. Towns took it, putting it in a separate pocket so as to make sure not to gamble it at any cost. They had to get up at six in the morning to make their plane and Towns promised to be back by two at the latest. He gave the boy a fresh icepack and went off to look for Bunny. He had always said that he could either take gambling or leave it, but now, for the first time in his life, he wasn't so confident about it. When he was in the area of a casino, there was no stopping him. He made sure to be in the area of one some four or five times a year. To a certain extent, when he was alone, he did get some pure pleasure out of gambling. He could sit down at a blackjack table at eight in the evening, get up at four in the morning, and not know what had happened to the time. Sipping brandies and pulling on a delicious cigar or two. Sometimes, when he was ahead, he would slip in a quick hooker and then saunter back to the tables. They had a new kind of semihooker in Vegas, dazed girls from Northern California who would straggle through Vegas on weekends to pick up some cash and then push on. Some were startling in their beauty and almost all were junkies. They were both better and worse than your normal Vegas hooks. They didn't hold you up on the price. It depended on whether you liked dazed and beautiful Northern California junkies or your died-in-the-wool Vegas showgirl types. This was at a time of his life when Harry Towns didn't think much about hookers. He just more or less took them on. That would change later. Of course, none of this applied if you had a son along. Ideally, it was not a good idea to have anyone along when you were gambling. Even a supportive girlfriend. It was a private thing to do and you had to concentrate. Besides, you had all the company you needed, right there at the table. And don't forget the dealer. And the cards.

As on all other nights when he was to win, Harry Towns started off dropping some. But then he made it back and when he went ahead, he began slowly to convert his five-dollar chips into twenty-fives until he was playing exclusively with the expensive chips. Half the fun of the twenty-fives was the extra attention you got from the other players; often you got a little crowd around you. By one in the morning, Harry Towns had a good stack of the high-priced chips; he counted them on the sly, considering it bush league to do it openly, and saw that he was ahead eleven hundred dollars. Anything over a thousand started to be "significant money" to Towns, who began to think of going ahead as much as five or even ten thousand. A comedian started to tell jokes to the crowd in a lounge behind Towns's table; he was sure this would throw him off, but it was one of those nights and he kept winning all the same. And he wasn't that good a player. For example, he never went out of his way to wait for the "anchor" seat where you could survey the board and have a somewhat better chance of predicting the next card to come up. He always took insurance which, statistically, was a bad bet. He just liked the idea of being insured. And he was too interested in the other players. If he saw a man with terrific hands, he would say, "I'll bet you work with your hands," and find out that the fellow was a champion three-wall handball player. So he would know that, but his attention would have been diverted for a split second, and that tended to widen the casino's edge.

He heard his name paged over the loudspeaker. He thought of leaving his chips where they were and telling the dealer to hold his place—in the style of the real gamblers—but when it came down to it he didn't trust the people at the table not to snatch some; so he gathered them up in his pockets and went to take the call. It was the boy on the hotel phone saying his father had promised to come back to the room at two. "I did, but it's only one-thirty," said Towns.

"No it isn't," said the boy, starting to cry. "It's later than that. It's almost morning. Look what you're doing to me." Towns said it really wasn't two yet, and could he please hold out until it was. "I know what I promised and I'm sticking to it. I'm winning a lot now." When he got back to the table, someone had taken his seat and he had to sit a few spots over on the end. Bunny smiled at him, as though he knew all about the boy with icepacks in the room. Towns bet heavily and indeed shocked himself by winning a few hundred more; but then, like a veteran fighter coming on in the late rounds, the dealer, with slow, kind, almost remorseful fingers, began inevitably to grind Towns down and take it all back. He took Towns's first-night winnings, the money he was ahead for the night, and five hundred more that he needed badly. When

Towns's last chip had been cleared, the dealer said, "One of those nights. I thought you had me there for a while."

"I didn't," said Towns. "The thing with me is that I need a lot of time. When I rush I get killed."

When he got back to the room, the boy was cranky and irritable and said his head was killing him. Towns easily matched him in irritability. "I was winning a bundle until you called me," he said. He tossed the boy his twenty-five dollars and said, "Anyway, here's your money. I didn't lose that."

"Yes, you did," said the boy. "And I don't want it." The boy started to cry and said, "I was dying in here and you were out there." Towns said he was sorry and that he would stay with him now. When the boy had cried himself to sleep, Towns smoked a cigarette in the dark, feeling very dramatic about it, and then went into the bathroom to see if his hair had grown back. There was a little shadow around his groin, but he could see that it was going to be a long haul. He checked to make sure the boy was sleeping and then went into the bathroom again where he made a long-distance call to the Bryn Mawr girl, paying no attention to what time of day or night it was in New York. She was drowsily awake and he told her about losing the money and what had happened to the boy. "And I've got body lice," he said. The girl laughed hysterically and when she had recovered for a moment she said, "You've got crabs. That's the funniest thing I've ever heard in my life." He knew it was going to be all right with her and that made him feel better; but when he came out of the bathroom and looked at the sleeping boy, he felt like a thief for having made a call to the girl when the kid was probably hoping and praying he would get back together with his mother. Towns couldn't sleep at all and decided the trip had been a bust. The dam, the bowling alley, dropping five hundred, and now bringing the kid back with a broken face.

The boy evidently didn't see it that way. He was cheerful when he awakened and said, "Do we have to go back today? I think I love Las Vegas more than anyplace in the world." That helped Towns out a little, but not much. "How come you loved it?" he asked. "We hardly did anything. And look what happened to your face."

"I can't explain it," said the boy, hugging his father. "I just loved it. And I wish we didn't have to go home."

Towns saw that the boy was really saying he had loved being away with his father, eating together, going places with him, anyplace at all, sleeping in the same hotel room. All that did was make Towns feel worse; he hated himself for not having shown the boy a better time, for having the crabs, for calling up Bryn Mawr girls in the middle of the night, for not knowing how to get back with the boy's mother. When they were packed, Towns settled his account at the front desk and noticed that the doctor's bill had been tacked onto it. They got a cab in front of the hotel and Towns told the driver to take them to the airport. "Oh hell," said the driver, his shoulders slumping. "I don't want to go to the airport." The boy looked at his father with a dumbfounded expression and then began to laugh so hard that Towns got worried about his cheekbone. "Where *would* you like to go?" Towns asked the driver, playing along for the boy's benefit. This time the child laughed so hard he had to hold his face which must have pained him. Towns knew the boy was on to a story he would talk about for years, a driver who only liked to go to places *he* wanted to go to. Towns and his son shared a whole bunch of those. The driver finally turned on the ignition and started off along the Strip. Towns put his arm around the child and asked him how he felt, and the boy said not too bad, but that the day he turned twenty-one he was going to come out to Las Vegas, maybe with a friend or two, so he could gamble. "That's a ways off," said Towns, but when he said it he realized it wasn't that far off after all. And that there wasn't too much time. Before he turned around, the boy would be in his teens, away at college, maybe in the service, and God knows what after that. With a divorce coming up, the time with the boy would probably be lumped into weekends and maybe a little bit of the summer. He wished, at that moment, he could start the Vegas trip all over again. If he could only do that, he would forget about the casino entirely and spend every second with the boy, and really show him a time. Maybe they *would* go camping. He'd buy a couple of sleeping bags and figure out a way to put up one of those fucking tents. When they got to the center of town and began to drive past some of the cheaper casinos, Towns suddenly told the driver to stop in front of one of them. "What for?" asked the driver. "Just stop," said Towns. He made sure to say it in a measured way so the driver would make no mistake about how serious he was. When the cab stopped, Towns got out with the boy and walked up to the cashier of a corner casino where he changed the boy's twenty-five dollars into quarters and halves.

"What's that for?" asked the boy.

"For you," said Towns. "To play the slots."

"I thought I wasn't allowed to," said the boy, standing in front of a quarter machine.

"Just play," said Towns.

"I don't know, Dad," said the boy. "What about him?"

He pointed to a uniformed man approaching them from the rear of the casino.

"I see him," said Towns.

"I don't feel right, Dad," said the boy, putting in his first quarter and pulling the lever.

"It's all right," said Towns. "Play." And he took a position with his back to the boy, his legs a fraction bent, his elbows close to his sides, as though he were cradling a machine gun and would kill any sonofabitch that dared to come within ten feet of the two of them.

③
HIGH, WIDE, and HANDSOME

Whenever Harry Towns ran into a new girl, sooner or later he would tell her that he lived in "a tower of steel and glass high above Manhattan." There is no record that any of them were impressed by this phrase. But he certainly liked the sound of it. The apartment was on the thirtieth floor of a new building in the middle of the city. The monthly rent was absurd, but Harry Towns took the place all the same, figuring he would worry about one month at a time. He would have the apartment and something would always come up to get him by. He had been in it nine months and something always had. "The only time I get into trouble," he would say, justifying his extravagance, "is when I bite off less than I can chew." He would say that to girls too, and they liked it about as much as the "tower of steel and glass" line.

He was a little afraid of being up so high. What if he got excruciatingly lonely one night or if he gave a little party and some freak dropped acid in his drink? He might want to make a leap for the pavement. So one of the things he did before signing the lease was to see if he could fit through a window. He tested one in the living room, getting an arm and part of his shoulder through, but that was as much of him as would fit. When he took the place, he noticed that you could see three bridges from the apartment and this was thrilling, but once he moved in the only time he ever checked the bridges was when the rent was due. He would look at them and feel a little better about the high monthly figure. Then there was the early-morning light. When the sun came up, it crashed through the dining alcove with such brilliance and ferocity you might have thought it would tear off a corner of the apartment. Harry Towns would like to have seen someone try to be gloomy in the face of that white and dazzling spectacle. Once he moved in, however, he saw very little of that time of day. He kept shaky hours and was usually dead asleep in the bedroom dark until noon. He loved the apartment so much he knew they would have to come in with guns to get him out of there, but it wasn't especially the light or the three bridges that turned the trick for him.

The furniture was part of it. He had never selected furniture before and his style in picking it out was fast and giddy. He would tell the "tower of steel and glass" girls that he had wrapped up the furniture purchase in five minutes and the truth was it probably had not taken him more than ten. When it was time to select a bed, the salesman winked and said, "I've got one big as a ballfield." It was, and Harry Towns grabbed it. In helping Towns with the decorative colors, the salesman used the first-person style of fight managers in describing their strategy to the press. "I'm going with basic white on the walls and then I plan to move my hot colors into a few of the living-room pieces." Towns left it all to him. The salesman said not to worry about the money, but on the day the furniture was delivered, he got very worried about it and would not leave without a check. Towns had enough money for it, but not much more. The furniture really was steel and glass with plenty of leather thrown in. It brought a clean smell to the place which had stayed in the air for all of the nine months he had lived there. Towns could not remember a day he hadn't enjoyed his furniture all over again. He would come in each day, smell it, sit in some of the chairs, and generally check around to see that the furniture was all right. Years back, when Towns worked in an office, he and a homosexual copywriter used to spend their lunch hours together in furniture stores, Towns's friend saying he would love to move right into one in particular and Towns agreeing it was a fine idea. It was Towns's most serious brush with homosexuality and it occurred to him that all of his new interest in decorating might be an echo of the old homosexual furniture-store lunches coming back to haunt him.

When a new girlfriend came up to his place, Towns put a lot of emphasis on what she thought of the way he had set it up. If she had some reservations, he would give her a low mark. It would take him a long time to warm up to her. An old friend, known for his savage honesty, appeared one night and, after looking around, said, "I have to tell you straight out, I don't like your furniture. You know me, I'm honest." Amazingly, Towns was not that hurt. He knew the fellow had a house in the suburbs with a black welcoming jockey on the front lawn. But throughout the evening he got the friend to try out different chairs, saying it was probably the kind of furniture that took some getting used to. "I'll bet you've changed your mind about the stuff," he said to the friend as he saw him off. "Not really," said the brutally honest fellow.

It was not just an apartment, of course; it was a whole building, with a sea of doormen, sub-doormen, and handymen, all standing around, none of them with that much to do. There were probably one and a half in help for each tenant and Towns felt an obligation to dream up assignments for them. One fellow would spot Towns approaching the building, as far as a block away, and dash out to help him with his packages, even if they were little ones. The fellow was whipped and hooked-over like an old bullfighter and Towns, strong as a mule in the shoulders, felt foolish accepting his help; but he sensed there was a point of pride involved and let the fellow have his head. Another doorman, who got cabs for Towns, leaped back and smacked his head in shock each time Towns gave him a tip, as if to say, "Holy God, I never expected this." There were special night men, too; the one who usually admitted Towns at four in the morning would clutch his collar tightly around the neck as he opened the front door, falling back as though a blizzard had swept in with Towns. He did this even on calm summer nights.

The building had a garage below it where Towns kept a car for the weekends when he hung around with his son. You could go from your apartment right to the garage and then sweep out into the night, all in one motion, without ever having the air hit you. That part made Towns feel like a racketeer. As a security measure, you got a special key to summon the garage elevator. If you didn't have the key, no soap, and you would be trapped out there in the hallway, presumably to be captured by building authorities. Towns liked the special key, but did not feel he needed all that security. As a matter of fact, he had often thought of mugging someone himself, just to get the feel of it and to turn the tables on the crime-in-the-streets issue. He actually picked out a little old man one night, but did not follow through. In any case, he felt he could take care of himself and wished the building would drop a little of the security and lower the rent a couple of bucks. Just after Towns moved in, a black garage man banged up his car. When Towns went to see him about it, the fellow said, "One thing I want with all my heart is to get into the FBI." Thrown off balance, Towns said, "I'll check around and see what I can do." For weeks, the assignment took up a space in Towns's mind and he was sorry he hadn't told the fellow straight out that he had no handle at the security organization. Each time he came for his car, the fellow asked, "Anything break yet?" to which Towns answered, "I'm still working on it." After a while, the fellow stopped asking and got Towns his car in a very sullen way. Towns finally gave him the number of a man who covered crime for a small New Jersey daily. "That's about as close as I could get," he said. "It won't work," said the garage man, handing back the number. But after that, he was a little more cheerful.

*   *   *

The first girl to visit Towns in his new apartment was an actress who took one look around and began to do musical-comedy production-number kicks in and out of the furniture. She took off her clothes and sat around on his new chairs naked; Towns could not get over his good fortune, but before long she was slumped over, weeping because she was unable "to get her shit together." She said the city had "put her into a heavy." All of this was acceptable to Towns so long as she didn't put her clothes back on. But the next day, he found little clumps of hair all over his new furniture. He kept finding them for a week after she was gone and even spotted some on the top shelf of his glass bookcase, wondering how they had gotten up there. Even though he loved her kicks, he decided not to have her back.

There was something about the apartment, no question about that. A friend of his, in the sweater business, who had once confessed to Towns that he could get it up but couldn't get it off, arrived one day, sat down on the couch and said, "If I lived here, I'm positive I could get it off." Towns was fond of saying that once he got a girl up to the apartment she was a dead duck. The truth is, he never knew. One girl, a secretary who took parts in porno flicks, turned up in a leather outfit and Towns was certain she was a shoo-in. But she sat in a corner, crossed her legs like a vise, and began to pump him for sexual fantasies she could act out with her boyfriend. They had done every one they could think of. When Towns said he never bothered with them, she angrily accused him of holding some back. He made one up about a Mandarin king and his concubine which seemed to tickle her and then he got her out of there.

Whenever a new girl came up to the apartment he

would snap shut the double lock and then stand at the door while she sniffed around like a puppy and got used to the place. No matter what her reaction to the setup, Towns would say, "I haven't really finished it yet." Then he would put on some saxophone music that sounded like the apartment to him. It was cool, dry, very much like the effect of cocaine. He had never come across a girl who didn't react well to the music; some jotted down the names of the selections so they could buy the records for themselves. He knew the saxophone player personally, a plain-looking, scholarly fellow who had admitted to Towns that he was very lonely. Sometimes Towns felt funny about using the lonely fellow to supply the musical background while he coaxed girls into bed. It bothered him, but it never really shook him up, so he used the music anyway.

Once a girl kicked off her shoes and got settled in, he would arrange the lighting in a soft way, sit down beside her on one of the soft leather chairs, and put his arm around her shoulders; together they would admire the view. Most of the girls lived in small apartments that faced out on back alleys and were trying to get rid of their roommates on the grounds of sloppiness and insensitivity. In a sense, Towns knew he was lording it over them with his view and his fine apartment, but he could not resist doing it anyway. If a girl said she was hungry, he would bring out a trayful of play foods—pâté, caviar, Camembert, English biscuits. He associated the apartment with that kind of food and never kept anything normal around, like a head of lettuce or a loaf of white bread. He did his actual eating on the outside. If a girl said she wanted to tidy up, he would direct her to the powder room. Inside was a very feminine mirror and some light, summery colognes. It made him wince that he had turned into the kind of fellow who had a powder room with colognes in it; surprisingly it did not go over that well with the girls. They used it, but never reported getting any particular kick out of it.

Once he had eased a girl into the bedroom, he would align the speakers of his stereo so that his friend's saxophone music could curl around and follow them in there. He had a drawerful of drugs for girls who preferred them, everything from simple grass right up to ones that were in the big leagues. Cocaine, for example. The evenings each represented new adventures to him and at the same time had a lovely sameness to them. It probably dated him, but he would always hold his breath and wait to be stunned by that magical time when a girl began to take off her clothes. Though his expression ranged from neutral to bored, he would say to himself, "Great God in heaven, she's actually taking them off." When was he ever going to get past that? He liked girls who took all their things into the bedroom with them and didn't spread themselves all over the apartment. The neatness promised a neat and quick getaway in the morning. At that time, many of the girls, stewardesses in particular, would stretch out their arms and expect to have long, delicious, stretchy breakfasts which they would prepare for him. In his way, Towns loved every girl who had ever been to his place, but he passed up a great many breakfasts because the truth was he wanted to have his apartment back again, all to himself.

To his knowledge, he had never done anything cruel to any of his visitors. Anyone in pursuit of being smacked around mentally or physically got pointed in another direction. Unless you wanted to call that cruel. Once he hid a wavering stewardess's blue jeans, but if she had really insisted on having them back, he would have produced them. On occasion, he would simply ask a new arrival, "Do you feel like fucking?" just as casually as he might ask her to try a new white wine. But he had to be in the mood to say a thing like that. If he ever planned it ahead, it wouldn't work out. A remark like that was about as close to an attack as he ever came. Unless his apartment was supposed to be an attack. But there were no locks on the doors that couldn't be snapped open. And he didn't lasso women in the street and smuggle them up there. If a girl didn't like one of the blunt remarks, she could just wheel around in a huff and take off. Some did. And a surprising number didn't. There was only one surefire time when Harry Towns could tell that a girl was going to slip away. Those were the times when he was down on himself. Women sniffed that out and didn't want any part of it. They still wanted men to be confident. Quietly confident, the way they were in the ads for small cigars. Towns was starting to like women who were confident, too. Everyone was looking for confidence and trying to grab onto it.

He tried not to make promises. All he had to offer was himself, whatever that was worth. And his apartment. For an evening or two. He wasn't delighted with that state of affairs, but that's the way it was for the time being. He tried to think of someone who could alter all that, someone he would want to stay on and on, but even in his mind, where all bets were off, or drawing from the films, he couldn't come up with anyone. The perfect woman would be a terrific one who would show up and leave and then reappear when he wanted her to. He couldn't see why anyone truly first-rate would want to go along with that.

Once he heard the line, "I'd like you to get to know me as a person," an alarm bell went off. He might just as well have been asked if he was a Capricorn. He wasn't ready for that quite yet. And the person he would like to get to know as a person wouldn't ask him quite that way. She would figure out another style. She would say, "I'd like you to get to know me as a yak." Something along those lines.

Only one friend got to hang around in the morning and to come back at least once a week, the Bryn Mawr girl who ran a laugh-sweetening machine at a TV studio, sliding laughs into comedy series with the machine. Towns felt he knew her as a person. He let her keep her slippers in his bedroom closet, though he kicked them deeper in when other girls came over to visit. The only trouble was that this special girl was afraid of his apartment. The first time she saw it, she rocked back and forth in a chair, holding the leather arms so fiercely that the veins on her arms bulged out. At first he was annoyed and said, "How can you be afraid of an apartment? I never heard of that."

"But I am," she said. Then he saw that she was really petrified and he was very tender with her. She said the cold, antiseptic atmosphere, the glass and steel he was so proud of, reminded her of a hospital ward. "That's because I haven't filled it in yet," he said. He bought some colorful rugs and pictures and each time she showed up he would ask her if it was beginning to warm up. "A little bit," she said. He was very fond of this girl and admired the fact that she stood on her own two feet and ran a laugh-sweetening machine. If it was a question of moving someone in, he would have chosen her. And she would have liked being chosen. But at the moment, all he really wanted was sole occupancy of that apartment he loved. He wanted to bring people in and then have them leave.

One day Harry Towns picked up his boy in the suburbs and brought him back to stay overnight in the apartment. The boy had trick knees and favored his mother around the cheekbones. "I didn't know it was going to be like this," said the boy, running in and making himself at home. "I thought my father would be in an old ratty place in the Bowery."

"I haven't really fixed it up yet," said Towns.

"What about this chair?" asked the boy, hopping on a white one and testing it out. "Do you own it?"

"Yes," said Towns.

"Holy cow," said the boy, socking his head and testing out another. "How about this one?"

"I own that one, too."

The boy tried out each piece of furniture, stopping to ask Towns if he owned it. Towns said he owned them all.

"Are you ever going to bring them home?" asked the boy.

"No," said Towns. "They go with the apartment." The boy was not really clear on the separation arrangement and Towns had never gotten around to filling him in on it. In truth, he wasn't too clear on it himself. Neither was his wife, evidently. At some point, Towns would have to take the lead and get it nailed down, but for the moment, all that could be said for sure was that he lived in one place and his wife and son lived in another.

"What happens when you're finished up here? Do you have to give all the chairs back?"

"No, I keep them. I really do own them."

There actually weren't any things for boys in the place

and Towns wound up showing his son a bunch of tools, an expensive set he had received as a gift. He didn't use them, but they looked fine and he liked having them around. "What are you showing me them for?" asked the boy.

"I thought you'd like to have a look at them," said Towns. "They were made in West Germany."

"Well, you don't have to show me things."

The boy checked the refrigerator and seemed puzzled by the tins of pâté and caviar and the triangles of Camembert. But then he found a bag of potato chips in the pantry and said, "What a setup. You've got everything here, Dad." Scooping up the bag, he turned on the TV set and settled in as though he had been living there for years.

Later, Towns went out for a while. Before he left, he tucked the boy into his bed, feeling a little funny about sticking him in there where all those stewardesses had been. But the sheets were fresh and clean so it was probably all right. The boy had brought along a pair of pajamas but for some reason he wanted to sleep in his clothes. "I think I'll just keep 'em on," he said and would not explain why. When Towns came back a few hours later, the boy popped open an eye and said a couple of young girls had called but wouldn't leave their names. "What do you mean 'young'?" asked Towns.

"They sounded young," said the boy.

"Well, they're just a couple of friends," said Towns.

He went to sleep on a couch in the living room, glad that he was getting some use out of the sleeping feature of the couch, since it had cost more than any of his other pieces. The next morning he took the boy out to an elegant restaurant for breakfast. It had a garden attached to it and seemed to cater to divorced fathers who had their sons in for the weekend. There were rows of these fathers, all sitting very erectly and talking in a dignified way to their sons who were exceptionally well-behaved. If you closed your eyes, you would not have thought there was a child in the place since the fathers talked to their boys as if they were fellow executives. They seemed to be hurrying their sons along to adulthood so they could fend for themselves and be free of the divorce atmosphere. The fathers all seemed to be terrifically sober, even-tempered fellows; Towns could not imagine why a wife would want to unload the worst of them. Most of them had thinning hair which may have been a factor.

Even though he tried not to be, Towns, in talking to the boy, was a little more dignified than preferred. The waiter, completely at ease in handling divorced kids, got a big breakfast out on the table, hot and in a hurry. That went over very well with Towns's kid, who graded restaurants on the basis of how fast they got the food out of the kitchen.

"What did you think of my new place?" Towns asked the boy.

"Great," said the boy, "except that I can hardly wait for you to finish up with it."

"I'm going to be there for a while," said Towns.

"Don't be there too long," said the boy. "I liked it much more when you were home every night and didn't have to spend all that time in the city."

You would think that Towns would not so much get tired of the apartment as start to take it for granted. After all, it was just a place to live, with some great furniture in it. But as the months rolled along, he found he loved it more and more. He loved the heating-and-cooling system and the specially sealed windows and would have sworn that not a grain of pollution ever sneaked in through them. City apartments were supposed to have paper-thin walls, but when Towns turned his favorite saxophone music up very high so he could really bathe in the music nobody made a fuss about it. The music seemed to pour out into the city instead of back into the building. Only when he sneezed did a far-off neighbor holler back, "God bless you." Towns had a powerful sneeze. The only tenant he ever said hello to was a fellow down the hall who wore bright Haitian outfits. One night, Towns and a stewardess went out into the carpeted halls naked just for the thrill of it. The door almost locked behind them and Towns had to dive at it, landing on his stomach, to keep it from closing. He had nightmares about what it would have been like to be caught out there naked in the halls. What would the fellow with the festive blouses have done if they had knocked on his door? He decided that his neighbor would have taken them in with great good humor while the door was being opened and not called in someone from the tabloids.

Sometimes it bothered him that he got such great enjoyment out of his apartment. What was he, some kind of apartment freak? Of course, he had never had one of his own before. He had leaped from his mother's house into the Army and then into being married, with no time between for being a guy on his own in an apartment; no question that had something to do with it. When the marriage went down the drain, he took what he called a "poor-student's place" that got knocked over regularly by junkies. On at least five occasions, he had come back to it to find the windows open, the curtains fluttering, and things missing. Not that he ever lost much. It was the terrible feeling of helplessness and violation that got right into the center of him. It got so bad he actually wanted to keep the doors and windows open as if to say, "Take anything you want. I don't care anymore." Amazingly, he got a lot of his screenwriting work done in this poor-student's apartment. He was just getting started with girls and found a few who went into a delighted heat over how tawdry it was. But it was not really his place. It belonged to a friend who had a great deal of material stored in crates and kept coming back at irregular intervals to take some of the crates out and put others back in. Towns wasn't even curious to know what was in them. In the new apartment, everything, right down to the last ashtray, belonged to Harry Towns. He did not complete any scripts in it, but that would come. All he got out of it was fierce pleasure.

One day Towns's wife called him and said she wanted to meet him for dinner. She seemed very nervous and got a piece of her salad stuck in her throat. He helped her by slapping her on the back and the salad piece finally went down, but it pretty much blew the dinner for her. He told her she looked very young and pretty; she picked up the young part, telling him she thought so, too, but did he *really* think so? Actually, she didn't look that young, but that had never been an issue with him. If it had gone well with them, he would have loved her, wrinkles and all. He would have loved being able to love someone with wrinkles. She took a brave swig of her drink and said that whatever she had to get out of her system she had gotten out and now the thing she wanted most in the world was for him to move back to the house and for them to be a family for as long as they lived. They had had a handful of these meetings before, but Towns believed this one though he had never bought the others. He said he thought it was terrific that she could say something like that to him, but that he wasn't at all sure he could go back to the arrangement she was proposing. He walked her to her car, wondering for a second if he ought to take her up to his apartment and then deciding it was the worst idea of the century. He kissed her good-bye and she said, "Remember, I'll be out there, not doing anything, not going anywhere, just waiting." He wished she hadn't said that to him. It struck him as being below the belt.

He went back to his apartment and for the first time he felt awful up there. He had had twinges of loneliness now and then and some uneasiness when he was not able to work, but there had been no way for him to feel seriously low in that place. It wasn't set up that way. Even when he was sick with a virus, he had had a pretty good time of it. She had put him in the position of having to say no to being together with his boy and a terrific wife. The terrific wife part was no joke, either. He had noticed a thin steady line of responsibility in her eyes and he trusted that. But it all had to do with giving up the apartment and each time he thought about that it seemed his stomach would drop like the building elevator. Who would move in and take it over—a sales representative? From Monsanto Chemicals? A couple of fag decorators? Of course he could keep the apartment and they could all use it together, but that idea seemed the worst he had come up with so far. No matter how responsible his wife's eyes looked, he did not want her up there with him and suddenly feeling a little depressed. No one was going to be a little depressed in his place. Unless it was him. Moving his old family in would have been like yanking all of those extraordinary past nights out of his life with a pliers.

After he saw his wife he felt some pressure to make a decision right that second. He was that way. What he decided was to pour himself a long Scotch on the rocks. Buying an elaborate bar had seemed an extravagance at the time, but now that he had it, it seemed to have been the absolutely right move. He put on some of his friend's saxophone music and sat down on a favorite leather chair with his legs stretched out. This time he really did examine the view and he decided that even if he only checked it once or twice a month it was important that he always have one. Even when he wasn't looking at it, he knew it was out there. He suddenly remembered a spinster aunt who was always falling in love with unattainable men, attractive, but described by the family as being "high, wide, and handsome." That struck him as being the best description of how he felt when he was in his apartment. He checked his answering service and found out that a girl named Harry had called, a stewardess he had met coming back from Baltimore. He had fed her some quick guru material, saying, "Your name's not Harry, it's Jane," explaining that if she really wanted to feel released and free of earthly concerns, it wouldn't matter to her whether she thought of herself as Harry or Jane. He didn't have time to work in much more, but she seemed delighted with the little bit he had handed her. Still, he had figured the odds against her calling were six to one against. It was like holding twelve at blackjack and drawing a nine to it. With a hundred bucks on the card. And did he love girls with boys' names! He called her back and made a date for later that evening, picking out a bar that was just a stone's throw from his apartment. Two drinks and he would have her up there with him, checking out the view. The date meant that he was covered for the evening and that now he could sit back and enjoy his favorite time of all, that confident space between now and the time he would pick her up. He would have another drink and then take a delicious nap in the tomblike quiet of his bedroom. No need to set the alarm. He would know when to get up. Then he would take a slow shower beneath one of the world's greatest needlepoint showerheads. If the building asked him for fifty bucks more a month for the privilege of having that showerhead he would have coughed it up without a murmur.

Now that he felt easier, he thought he saw it all pretty sharply. His wife would never believe it in a million years, but it wasn't the girls so much. It was the apartment and the way he felt up there. He wanted to watch the boy grow and shoot baskets with him and particularly to sit with him at the doctor's office and see that he got the very best care for his knees and that no one gave him the runaround. (The doctor was treating a famed big-league pitcher, only you weren't supposed to let on that you knew this. You were supposed to pretend he was just another doctor.) And Towns wanted a family to sit around with and to take on great vacations to places he had never been. Places like Portugal. He wanted to stand around on a lawn in the country and plant things. Sometimes he wanted all these things so much it was like a physical ache.

But leave this place? Leave the furniture, the clean smell, the doormen, the special garage with its special key? The view that let you see not one but three bridges if you wanted to? Actually pull out? Leave the girls named Harry? The Kathies and Susies with their long straight fragrant hair and the new style that no longer said I won't kiss you until the second date—the way it was in Towns's day—but had graduated to I won't sleep with you until the second date. And there was a way to get around that, too. Say good-bye to it? The only place in the world where he had ever been totally relaxed, private, confident, king of the city? No past, no hassle, plenty of time, exactly the way those out-of-reach mustached boyfriends of his spinster aunt must have felt—high, wide and handsome? Walk away from it? For what? A kid with bum knees, a house in the sticks, and a wife with a good fifteen years on the oldest cupcake he had ever let through the door?

No way. But he did have to sit there and laugh for a while at the way he had actually considered the idea. Even for a split second. He must be some patsy.

④
LaDY

When it was good, it was of a smooth consistency and white as Christmas snow. If Harry Towns had a slim silver-foil packet of it against his thigh—which he did two or three nights a week—he felt rich and fortified, almost as though he were carrying a gun. It was called coke, never cocaine. A dealer, one side of whose face was terrific, the other collapsed, like a bad cake, had told him it was known as "lady." That tickled Harry Towns and he was dying to call it that, but he was waiting for the right time. The nickname had to do with the fact that ladies, once they took a taste of the drug, instantly became coke lovers and could not get enough of it. Also, they never quite got the hang of how expensive it was and were known to toss it around carelessly, scattering gusts of it in

the carpeting. Even though one side of his face was collapsed, the dealer claimed there were half-a-dozen girls
who hung around him and slept with him so they could
have a shot at his coke. Harry Towns could not claim to
have enslaved groups of women with the drug, but it did
help him along with one outrageously young girl who
stayed over with him an entire night. She didn't sleep with
him, but just getting her to stay over was erotic and something of an accomplishment. Wearing blue jeans and
nailed to him by the sharp bones of her behind, she sat on
his lap while he fed her tastes of it all night long. She
lapped it up like a kitten and in the morning he drove her
to her high-school math class. He wasn't sure if he was
proud of this exploit—she wasn't much older than his
son—but he didn't worry about it much either.

If someone asked Harry Towns to describe the effects
of coke, he would say it was subtle and leave it at that. He
could remember the precise moment he had first smelled
and then tried grass—a party, a girl in a raincoat whose
long hair literally brushed the floor, some bossa nova
music that was in vogue at the time, a feeling he wanted
to be rid of both his wife and the tweed suit he was
wearing—but he could not for the life of him figure out
when coke had come into the picture. It had to do with
two friends in the beginning, and he was sure now that
the running around and hunting it down was just as
important as the drug itself. They would spend a long
time at a bar waiting for someone to show up with a
spoon, one of them leaping up at regular intervals to
make a call and see if their man was on his way. It was
exciting and it kept them together. While they were waiting, they would tell each other stories about coke they had
either heard about or tried personally, coke that was like a

blow on the head, coke that came untouched from the drug companies, coke so strong it was used in cataract eye operations. Or they would tell of rich guys who gave parties and kept flowerpots full of it for the guests to dip into at will. It was a little like sitting around and talking about great baseball catches. Sometimes they wondered how long you could keep at it before it began working on your brain. Even though they kidded about winding up years later in the back streets of Marseilles with their noses chewed away, it was a serious worry. Freud had supposedly been an addict and this buoyed them up a bit. Also, Towns had once run into a fellow who lived in Venezuela most of the year and had a gold ring in his ear. Rumor had it that he was a jungle fag. Leaning across to Towns one night, he had tapped his right nostril, saying "This one's thirty-six years old." The fellow was a bit bleary-eyed, but otherwise seemed in good health; the disclosure was comforting to Towns although he wondered why the fellow said nothing about his left nostril.

Once their contact arrived, they would each get up some money, not paying too much attention to who paid the most. Then they would go into the bathroom, secure the door, and lovingly help one another to take snorts from the little packet. One of Towns's friends was a tall stylish fellow who was terrific at wearing clothes, somehow getting the most threadbare jackets to look elegant. It was probably his disdainful attitude that brought off the old jackets. The other friend was a film cutter with a large menacing neck and a background in sports that could not quite be pinned down. They were casual about dividing up the drug, with no thought to anyone's being short-changed, although later on, the stylish fellow would be accused of having a vacuum cleaner for a nose. But it was a sort of good-natured accusation. On each occasion, Towns's debonair friend could be counted on to introduce a new technique for getting at the coke, putting some in a little canal between two fingers, getting a dab of it at the end of a penknife, and on one occasion producing a tiny, carved monkey's paw, perfectly designed to hold a little simian scoopful. Towns's favorite approach was the penknife one. The white crystals, iced and sparkling, piled up on the edge of the blade, struck him as being dangerously beautiful. But Towns felt with some comfort that the varied techniques placed his friend farther along the road to serious addiction than he was; Towns made do with whatever was on hand, usually the edge of a book of matches, folded in half. The film cutter had a large family, and occasionally they would tease him about his children having to eat hot dogs because of his expensive coke habit. One night he gave them both a look and they abandoned that particular needle. He had been ill recently, and they had heard that four hospital attendants had been unable to hold him down and give him an injection.

After they had taken their snorts, they would each fall back against the wall of the john and let the magic drip through them, saying things like "Oh, brother," and "This has got to be the best." Towns usually capped off the dreamily appreciative remarks by saying, "I'll always have to have this." The stocky film cutter admitted one night that if it came to choosing between the drug and a beautiful girl, he would have to go with the coke. It seemed to be a painful admission for him to make, so Towns and the debonair fellow quickly assured him they both felt exactly the same way. Actually, Towns didn't see why one had to cancel out the other. He had heard that lovers would receive the world's most erotic sensation by putting dabs of coke on their genitals and then swiping it off. He tried this one night with a stewardess from an obscure and thinly publicized airline and found it all right, but nothing to write home about. As far as he could see, it was just a tricky way to get at the coke.

They would take about two tastes apiece and then bounce back into the bar with sly grins and the brisk little nose sniffs that distinguished the experienced coke user. Even if they scattered and sat with different people, the drug held them bound together in a ring. Later, when the evening took a dip, one of them would give a sign and they would return to the john to finish off the packet.

They kept their circle tightly closed, even though at least one fellow was dying to get into it. He was a writer who stood careful guard over his work and on more than one occasion had said, "I'll be damned if I'm going to let anyone monkey around with my prose." He also spoke of having "boffed" a great many girls. Towns took objection to that word "boffed" and so did his friends. They doubted that he had really done that much "boffing" and they didn't care that much for his prose either. So even though the fellow knew what they were doing in the john and gave them hungry, poignant looks, they would not let him into the group.

Sometimes, instead of waiting around at the bar, they would make forays into the night to round up some of the drug. They spent a lot of time waiting outside basement apartments in Chinatown, checking over their shoulders for the police. Towns owned the car and he had plenty of dents in the side to prove it. Somehow, tranquil and frozen by the drug, Towns felt that a little sideswipe here and there didn't matter much, but the dents were piling up and the car was pretty battered. The dapper, arrogant fellow sat in the back and seemed annoyed at having to ride around in such a disreputable-looking vehicle. He lived with his mother who supposedly did all his driving for him, after first propping him up beside her with blankets over his knees for warmth. Towns decided to have all the car dents fixed in one swipe and then start over.

Leaving his friends behind one night, Towns went on a drug-hunting foray with a hooker who had seemed beautiful in the saloon light, but turned out to be a heavy user of facial creams. He didn't object to a girl using creams in private, but felt she had an obligation to take them off when she was out and around. She said she knew of some great stuff just over the bridge in Brooklyn. Towns drove and drove and when he asked her if they were there yet, she said it was just a little bit farther. He felt he might as well be driving to Chicago. When they finally got the coke, she described herself, with some pride, as a "nose freak" —as though Towns would be thrilled to hear this. Then she got rid of most of the coke in the car, under a street lamp, leaving Towns with just a few grains. He felt it would be the right thing on his part to smack her around a little for her behavior, but he was worried about friends of hers running out of a nearby building with kitchen knives. So he let it pass. Besides, there had been something attractively illicit about snorting the drug with a heavily creamed hooker deep in the bowels of Brooklyn. And it was strong, too, even if there wasn't much of it. He would have something to say to his friends about "Brooklyn coke" and how it could tear your head off if you didn't watch it. So instead of smacking her around, he took her on a long, silent drive back to Manhattan where he let her out.

In the beginning, Towns and his friends would fool themselves into thinking that the nighttime get-togethers were for the purpose of having some dinner. They would polish off a Chinese dinner, and one of them would casually ask if the others felt like going after some coke. But after a while, they dropped all pretense, skipping the dinners and diving right into the business of getting at the drug. Towns soon discovered that he was throwing over entire evenings to phone calls, long waits, nervous foot-tapping, and great outbursts of relief when their man finally showed up with the prize. He wasn't sure if he felt the tension legitimately or if he was just playing at it. There weren't too many things in life he liked to do more than once in exactly the same way and he figured out that he was having the same kind of evening over and over. So one night he simply stopped, probably too cruelly and abruptly, the way he stopped most things. He decided to get a whole bunch of coke and have it just for himself. He invited the dealer with the collapsing face up to his apartment and told him to bring along an entire ounce. It was a very exciting and significant call for him to make, and he rated it right up there with such decisions as moving out on his wife and signing up for a preposterously expensive apartment. Both had worked out. As soon as he called the dealer, he became afraid of some vague unnameable violence. His way of handling it was to strip down to his waist and greet the dealer bare-chested. Towns had a strong body and this maneuver would indicate that he was loose and could take care of things, even stripped down that way and obviously having no weapons concealed in the folds of his clothing.

The dealer didn't notice any of this. He swept right in and began to carry on about some new moisture-proof bottles he had found for the coke. If you closed them after snorts, no moisture would get in and the drug would not cake up. He was terribly proud of the bottles and told Towns to hang on to them; when they were empty, he would come by with refills. After he had left, Towns sank back on a leather chair and didn't even try any of the coke. He just lit a cigar and richly enjoyed having bottles of it up there on the thirtieth floor with him. The idea fell into his head that if you had a lot of it, you were relieved of the pressure of always having to get it and as a result you didn't take that much. But he got on to himself in a second and knew it wasn't going to work out that way. He'd take more. The next time he saw his friends they tried to start up the coke-hunting apparatus and he excused himself by saying, "I don't think I'm in the mood for any tonight." He felt very sorry for them; they would have to go to all that trouble for just a little packet of it that would be sniffed up in an evening. Somehow they sensed he had a whole bunch of coke of his own and were snappish with him, but they stopped that quickly because they weren't that way. The stylish fellow's eyes began darting all over the place and Towns sensed he was making plans to lay in a giant supply of his own. He would be all right. But the film cutter's head drooped and when he was alone with Towns, he admitted for the first time that even though he had many children, he hated his wife. The evenings of hunting down coke had been terribly important to him. He said he always knew Towns was afraid to get close to people and amazingly he started to cry for a few seconds. At that moment, Towns would have taken him up to the apartment and given him half of the huge amount of coke. It was a close call, and the next day he was thrilled that he hadn't. As to Towns's inability to stay close to people, the fellow probably had him dead right. He had gone with a girl for three years and then brutally chopped off the affair, practically overnight. When it came to girls, if there was going to be any chopping off, he wanted to be the one to do it. Once it had been the other way. He saw himself as a man who had gotten off to a shaky start, then patched himself together and now had tough scar tissue at the seams. Chopping . . . getting chopped off . . . what he hoped for in life was to work his way back to some middle path.

Meanwhile, he had all that coke and a whole new style of evening set up. He would spread some of the drug on a dark surface, a pretzel box as a matter of fact, snort some, rub a little on his gums, and then take a long time getting dressed, returning from time to time to the pretzel box for additional sniffs. The feeling in coke circles was that your aim in returning to the drug throughout an evening was to chase that original high. Speaking for himself, Towns saw his repeat trips to the pretzel box as a means of making sure his feet never got back on the ground. It may have added up to the identical thing. He had some special phonograph records that seemed to go with the coke, ones that he rarely changed. They seemed to deepen the effects of the drug; cigars helped to string out the sensation, too, and he felt he was the only one who knew this. When he was ready to go out, he would sprinkle some coke in tinfoil and try to figure out the best pocket to put it in, one he wouldn't forget and the least likely one for a federal agent to suddenly thrust his hand into and nail him on the spot. (A dealer once told him "There's no good pocket.") He would be able to return to the tinfoil for little tastes throughout the night and there would be enough in there, too, for friends he might run across. Doling out coke from the thin little packet would make him seem generous; at the same time, no one had to know about the moisture-proof bottles lined up and waiting for him back at his apartment.

It was amazing how little he worried about the illegality of what he was doing. Only once did this come home to him with any force. He was in a cocktail lounge in Vegas with two girls and for the life of him he couldn't figure out if they were hookers. He was only fair at determining things like that. Sometimes his actions were sudden and dramatic, and on this occasion, he reached out and stuck a fingerful of coke in each of their mouths, as if this would smoke them out and tell him if they were joy dolls. They both sucked on the fingers and loved what was happening, but Towns looked around the lounge and became aware of a number of men with white socks, shaved necks, and even expressions who appeared not to approve of his having traipsed in with more than one girl. They probably didn't go for his beard much, either. At least that's the impression he got. All of this shook him up. What if one of the girls suddenly hollered out, "He shoved coke in my mouth." Towns had a lawyer who was terrific in the civil liberties department, but he wasn't sure he could count on the fellow dashing out to Nevada on his behalf. He told the girls to wait for him, he had a lucky roulette hunch, and then he sneaked out of the casino and went to another one.

He didn't feel the danger much in the city, though. "Rich" is the only word to describe how he felt. When he started out of his apartment, high and immunized, he felt that nothing great had to happen. He didn't even have to wind up with a girl. The way he figured it, enough that was great had already happened. Right around the pretzel box. He knew there must be a dark side to all this, but he would worry about that later.

One of the smart things he did was not use his car. He had had enough of the sideswipes. In his new routine, going about on foot and using cabs, he would hit a few warm-up places where he knew some people and felt cozy and secure; then he would head for a drugged and adventurous bar that could always be counted on for packs of long-haired girls, each of whom for some reason had just left her "old man" or walked out on a waitressing job that very day. In the drugged atmosphere of this bar, it was possible to slip into these packs of girls and on occasion, to pick one off. All of a sudden he would be talking to one, and if her eyes looked right, asking if she would like to have a little coke in the john. If she said yes, he knew the battle was over and he was going to wind up in bed with her. The two went together. In his way, he was using the coke to push people around. One night, at one of the early bars, he stood next to two black men; one liked him, the other, whose glasses gave him the look of an abstract educational puzzle, didn't. He said that even though Towns was bigger than he was, he was positive he could take him outside and beat the shit out of him. Unlike liquor, the coke always had a defusing effect on Towns, who simply shrugged and said, "No way." Then, perhaps to teach the puzzle man a lesson, he invited the other black man into the john for some coke. They took some together and then the angry abstracted fellow appeared. Towns hesitated long enough to make his point and then gave him some, too. He put his arm around Towns and hugged him and Towns felt a little sad about how easy it had been to peel away his anger. Back at the bar, he got angry again and finally walked out in what seemed to be a flash of hot abstract lightning. His renewed fury made Towns feel a little easier. But you certainly could do things with that coke. One night, when Towns had failed to pry any of the girls loose from her pack, he went looking for a hooker and found a terrific one on the street who looked like a high-school cheerleader. She had a tough style and needled him, saying she had balled every guy in the city, so why not him? At one time this would have been a threat to Harry Towns, but it wasn't now. What did all those other guys have to do with him? She said they could go upstairs to a tragic-looking little hotel across the street and Towns said no deal, he wanted to take her to his place. She said there was no way on earth she would go to a stranger's apartment, and then he mentioned the coke. "Jesus, do you really have some?" she wanted to know. "Pounds of it," he said, "at my place." It was amazing. As tough and streetwise as she was, she jumped in a cab with him and off they went. And all he had done was *say* he'd had the coke. It was a weapon all right.

Sometimes, when he got finessed into drinking a lot, the liquor and drug combination left him shaky the next day. He had to make sure to let entire days go by without using any of the drug. On the off days, it would be like having a terrific date to look forward to. One night, a fellow with a beltful of tools walked up to Towns and said that if he ever saw him with his wife again, he would kill him in an alley. "We can do it now," said the fellow, with surprising politeness, "or at a time of your convenience." Towns could not pinpoint the wife in question, but he had a pretty good inkling of who she was. He felt weak and anesthetized, his limbs sluggish, caught in heavy syrup. He mumbled something and hoped the fellow wouldn't use the tools on him. So it wasn't all roses. He had to watch that sort of thing. Then, too, the moisture-proof bottles emptied out after a while and he had to get them filled up again. He made an appointment to go to the dealer's apartment this time, and when he got there, the fellow snatched up his money and sat him down next to a young blonde carhop-style girl who looked as though she had just given up thumb-sucking. Then he slid a huge switchblade with a capsule of amyl nitrite on it between them, and excused himself, saying he had to get the coke, which was a few blocks away. Towns knew about the capsule; it was for cracking open and sniffing. You got a quick high-voltage sexual rush out of it. He had graduated from it some time back and felt it was small potatoes next to coke. But what about having it on a switchblade with a yellow-haired teenager on the other side? It reminded Towns of a religious ceremony in which a hotly peppered herb was placed beside something delicious to remind worshippers of the hard and easy times of their forebears. But this seemed to be a kind of drug ritual, and he couldn't decide what his next move was supposed to be. Was he supposed to make a quick grab for the capsule and crack it open before she got at him with the switchblade? He decided to stick to light conversation.

A bit later, Towns excused himself to go to the john and by mistake opened the door to a closet; rifles and handguns came pouring out on him in a great metallic shower—as well as a few bullwhips. "Look what you did," said the girl, coming over in a pout, as though the cat had spilled some milk. Towns helped her to gather up the weapons; it seemed important to get them back in before the dealer returned. He showed up half an hour later, telling Towns that he was in great luck because he had come up with some pure coke rocks, much more lethal than anything Towns had been involved with before. This type of coke came in around once a year, something like softshell crabs; rich Peruvians sat around on their ranches and shaved slivers of it from a huge rock, inhaling these slivers for weeks on end and getting heart trouble in their thirties. But Towns wasn't to worry about this, since he would only be getting this one shipment and maybe never get a shot at it again. Another thing that wasn't to bother Towns was that the moisture-proof bottles would not be filled to the top this time. That was because the Peruvian coke rocks were so pure. Towns wasn't so sure about this. "Oh well," said the dealer, disdainfully, "if you want me to fluff them up." Towns thought of the weapons closet and decided to pass on this and get going. In a kind of furious between-the-acts blur of activity, the dealer and his girl whipped out armloads of equipment, and before Towns could make a move toward the door, the dealer had wound a rubber coil around his arm and was straining to make a vein pop up. Meanwhile, the girl was melting down a Peruvian rock, probably one that belonged to Towns, in a tiny pan. They were like a crack surgical team. So this was the famous shooting-up routine. Towns had never seen it and had always been curious about it. The dealer, one side of his face not only collapsing but running down, like oil on a canvas, plunged a hypodermic into his vein and went into a series of ecstatic shivers, at the same time keeping up a surprisingly sober running commentary for Towns: "What's happening is that I'm getting a rush twenty times more powerful than you get taking it up through your nose. This is really something.

The only trouble is, it will stop in about five minutes and I'll have to do it again. I've gotten so I can do it ten, twenty times, all through the night." None of this was appealing to Towns. He realized that the tableau was for his benefit, to hook him into the team so that he would wind up melting rocks with them in the tiny frying pan. It wasn't going to happen. There were certain things that he could say for sure he wasn't ever going to do—like skydiving—and this was one of them. When the dealer finished up his shivers, it was time for the girl to take her turn; that's what Towns wanted to be on hand to see. She stuck some equipment under her arm and said she was going off to do it privately. Towns felt around in his bottle and pulled out a good-sized rock, saying it was hers if he could watch her in action. "No way," she said, giving him an infuriated look, "that's one thing no one in the world is ever going to see." What she seemed to want to get across was that she had been through a thousand assorted hells but was going to keep this one area stubbornly cordoned off to herself. Towns shrugged good-naturedly as if to say, "Oh well, win some, lose some," but he felt the loss sharply and didn't even wait around to see her when she got back. That wasn't what he wanted. He thanked the shivering fellow for the Peruvian rocks and sauntered outside, deciding to hunt down another arrangement, one with less danger in the air.

He went through quite a few of these dealers. They tended to live in lofts and to have young, sluggish girl-friends; each was trying to "get something going" in the record business. The coke, according to them, was just a sideline. After Towns got his coke, he would be asked to listen to one of their tape decks. Not once did he like what he heard, even taking into account that he was not in a musical mood when he made these visits and just wanted to get the coke and get the hell out of there. It was his view that each of these fellows was going to fare much better as a coke dealer than as a musician. Towns's favorite dealer was a tall, agreeable chap who had once worked at the Mayo Clinic as a counselor. He had a healing, therapeutic style of selling the coke; after each buy, Towns would flirt with the idea of sticking around for a little counseling, although he never followed through. One day, the fellow announced that in order to kick his own coke habit, which was becoming punishingly expensive, he was making his first visit to London. That struck Towns as being on the naïve side. How could you get away from coke in London? Some faraway island would seem to be more the ticket, but the fellow had his mind made up on the British Isles and there was no stopping him. Towns was convinced they would have him picked off as a user the second he stepped off the plane and be ready and waiting to sell him some.

Dealers brushed in and out of Towns's life, and he could not imagine wanting some coke and not being able to come up with it. Yet that would happen on occasion, even though he started out early in the evening trying to drum some up. He had always told himself that all he had to do in that situation was have a few drinks and he would be fine. But he wasn't that fine. He would sit around at one of his spots and drum his fingers on the bar, uneasy and unhappy. Was he hooked? He had heard that when a famed racketeer was buried, friends of his, for old time's sake, had stuck a few spoons of first-grade coke in there with him, since the racket man had been a user. Once, high and dry at four in the morning, Towns actually found himself wondering if it would be possible to dig up the fellow and get at the coke. It all depended on whether it was in the coffin with him or on the topsoil somewhere. Towns wasn't sure of the details. If he knew for sure it was in the topsoil, he might have found a shovel somewhere in the city, driven out to the cemetery and taken a try at it. That's how badly he wanted it sometimes.

One day Towns got word that his mother had died. It did not come around behind him and hit him on the head, since the death had been going on for a long time and it was just a matter of waiting for the phone call. It had always been his notion that when he got this particular news, he would drive up to a summer resort his mother used to take him to each September and hang out there for a weekend, sitting at the bar, tracing her presence, thinking through the fine times they had spent together. That would be his style of mourning. But now that he had the news, he didn't feel much like doing that. Maybe he would later. Instead, he sat in his apartment, thirty floors over the city, and tried to cry, but he could not drum up any tears. He was sure they would come later, in some oblique way, so he didn't worry too much about it. He knew himself and knew that he only cried when things sneaked up on him. Then he could cry with the best of them.

His mother was going to be put in a temporary coffin while the real one was being set up. And she would be lying in the chapel from six to eight that evening, with the family receiving close friends; the following day she would be buried. It presented a bit of a conflict for Towns. At six o'clock, he also had an appointment to meet Ramos, an old friend who had come in from California the night before. Formerly an advertising man, Ramos had now gone over entirely to an Old-West style. Long-faced, sleepy-eyed, he turned up in the city looking as though he had ridden for days through the Funeral Mountains on a burro, seeking cowpoke work. He had taken Towns into the coatroom of the bar at which they met, pulled out a leather pouch that might have contained gold dust, and given Towns a sniff of some of the purest coke he had ever run across. It rocketed back and flicked against a distant section in the back of his head that may never have been touched before. Now Harry Towns had a new story to tell his friends about Western coke, the wildest and most rambunctious of all. And he wanted that place in the back of his head to be flicked at again. So they made an appointment for six o'clock the following evening to go and get some more. Except that now Towns had to be at the chapel with his dead mother. He wondered, soon after he heard about the loss, if he would keep the appointment with Ramos, and even as he wondered, he knew he would. He didn't even have to turn it over in his mind. After all, it wasn't the funeral. That would make it an entirely different story. It was just a kind of chapel reception and if he turned up half an hour late, it would not be any great crime. And he would have the coke.

Harry Towns was at the midtown bar to meet Ramos at six on the dot, hoping to make a quick score and then hotfoot it over to the chapel. But Ramos loped in some twenty minutes late, squinty-eyed, muttering something about the sun having crossed him up on the time. He had never even heard of the sun when he was in advertising. He sat down, stretched his legs, and tried to get Towns into a talk about the essential dignity of man, even man as he existed in the big city. Towns felt he had to cut him off on that. People were already pouring into the chapel. At the same time, he didn't want to be rude to Ramos and risk blowing the transaction. He told Ramos about his mother, and the man from the West said he understood, no problem, except that he himself did not have the coke. It was just up the street a few blocks at a divorced girl's house. They would just have one drink and get going.

The divorced girl lived in a richly furnished high-rise apartment with animal skins on the floor. Towns had to walk carefully to keep from sticking his feet in their jaws. She had racks of fake bookshelves, too, suspense-novel types that whirled around when you pressed a button and had coke concealed on the other side. He was certain she was going to turn out to be his favorite dealer. Long-legged, freshly divorced, she hugged Ramos, Towns wondering how they knew each other. The animal skins may have been some sort of bridge between them. More likely, they were teammates dating back to Ramos's advertising days. She also seemed interested in Towns, handing him a powder box filled with coke, something he had always dreamed of. He got the idea that this wasn't even the coke he would be buying. It was a kind of guest coke, a getting-acquainted supply. An hors d'oeuvre. That's what he called falling into something. But what a time to be falling into it. She told him to dig in, help himself, and they could take care of their business a bit later. The girl had legs that went on and on and wouldn't quit. Why had anyone divorced her? She went over to fiddle with some elaborate stereo equipment and Towns put the powder box on his lap and took a deep snort as instructed.

"Jesus Christ," she said, pressing the palm of one hand to the side of her head, "what in the hell are you doing?"

"You told me to dig in," he said.

"Yes, but I didn't know we had a piggy here."

"Don't tell someone to dig in if you don't mean it."

Now Towns really felt foolish. There was no way to proceed from the piggy insult, which bit deep, to buying half an ounce of the drug. So he had blown at least half the chapel service and he wasn't even going to get the coke. He vowed then and there to deal only with the tape-deck boys in their lofts. Ramos tried to smooth things over by telling her, "He's a true man," but she was breathing hard and there seemed no way to calm her down. "What a toke," she said. "I've seen people take tokes, but this one, wow."

"My mother just died," said Towns. As he said it, he knew he was going to regret that remark for a long time, if not for the rest of his life. He had once seen a fellow get down on his knees to lick a few grains of coke from the bottom of a urinal. That fellow was a king compared to Harry Towns—using his mother's dead body to get him out of a jam. And it got him out, too. "Oh God," said the girl, putting a comforting arm around Towns's shoulder, "I don't know how to handle death." Towns just couldn't wait any longer. He gave Ramos the money, told him to buy some coke from the girl and he would meet him later, after the chapel service. Then he got into a cab and told the driver to please get him across town as fast as possible. It was an emergency. You could travel only so fast in city traffic, and Towns got it arranged in his mind that it was the cabbie's fault he was getting there so late. He arrived at a quarter to eight, with only fifteen minutes left to the service. Some remnants of his family were there, and a few scattered friends. Also his mother, off to one side, in the temporary coffin.

Towns's aunt and his older brother were relieved to see him, but they didn't bawl him out. He would always appreciate that. They said they thought he might have been hurt and left it at that. What seemed to concern them most was the presence of a woman Towns's mother hadn't cared for. They couldn't get over how ironic it was that the disliked woman had turned up at the chapel. The few surviving members of Towns's family were very short and for the hundredth time, he wondered how he had gotten to be so tall. He chatted with some neighborhood friends of his mother, keeping a wary eye on the woman she hadn't liked. If Towns hadn't felt so low about showing up late, he might very well have chucked her out of there. A chapel official said the family's time was up. He gave out a few details about the funeral that was coming up the next day. The family filed out, and just as Towns was the last one to arrive, he was the last to leave, stopping for a moment at his mother's temporary coffin. He never should have worried about crying. Once he started, he cried like a sonofabitch. He probably set a chapel record. He cried from the tension, he cried from grief, he cried from the cab ride, from his coke habit, from the piggy insult, from his mother having to be cramped up in a temporary coffin and then shifted over to a real one when it was ready. They had a hard time getting him out of there.

That night, Ramos came by with the coke. Towns didn't weigh it, look at it, measure it. He never did. It seemed like a fat pack and he guessed that the girl had given him a good count because of the death. The main thing was that it was in there. He gave Ramos some of it, which was

97

protocol, and told him he would see him around. "I'll
stick with you, man," said Ramos, but Towns said he
would rather be alone. He didn't want people saying
"man" to him and telling him he had "a terrific head." All
of which Ramos was capable of. The coke had a per-
fumed scent to it, a little like the fragrance of the divorcee. Had she rubbed some of it against herself? His
guess was that she had. He took a snort of it, got into his
bathrobe, and put on some Broadway show music, the
kind his mother liked. The music would be the equivalent
of driving up to the old summer resort. But it didn't work.
It didn't go with the coke. During his mother's illness, he
had put her up in his apartment and moved into a hotel,
the idea being that she would get to enjoy the steel and
glass and the view and the doorman service. But she
didn't go with the apartment either, and they both knew
it. She stayed there a few weeks, probably for his sake, to
ease his mind about not having sent her away on lavish
trips, and then she said she wanted to go back to her own
home. She left without a trace, except for some sugar
packets she had taken from a nearby restaurant and put
in his sugar jar. To give him some extra and free sugar.
He wondered if he should go over and take a look at the
sugar. He was positive that it would start him crying
again, but he didn't want to do that just then. He could
always look at the sugar. Instead, he switched on some
appropriate coke music, took another snort of the drug,
and stared out at his view of the city, the glassed-in one
that was costing him an arm and a leg each month. His
mother had made a tremendous fuss over this view, but
once again it was for his sake. She had been very ill and
wanted to be in her own apartment. Staying in his had
been a last little gift for him, allowing him to do some-

thing for her. He kept the tinfoil packet of coke open beside him and he knew that he was going to stay where he was until dawn. He was not a trees-and-sunset man, but he liked to be around for that precise time when the night crumbled and the new day got started. He liked to get ready for that moment by snorting coke, letting the drug drive him a hundred times higher than the thirtieth floor on which he lived. Once or twice, he wondered about the other people who were watching that moment, if there were any. It was probably only a few diplomats and a couple of hookers. Normally, he would take a snort, luxuriate in it, and wait for a noticeable dip in his mood before he took the next one. This time he didn't wait for the dips. Before they started, he headed them off with more snorts. He saw now that his goal was to get rid of the entire half ounce before dawn. Never mind about the problem of coming down. He would take a hot bath, some Valium. He'd punch himself in the jaw if necessary, ram his head against the bathroom tile if he had to. The main thing was to have nothing left by the time it was dawn so he could be starting out clean on the day of the funeral. Then, no matter what he was offered, he would turn it down. He didn't care what it was, Brooklyn coke, Western coke, Peruvian coke rocks, coke out of Central Harlem. If someone gave him stuff that came out of an intensive-care unit, coke that had been used for goddamn brain surgery, he would pass it right by. Because the chapel was one thing. But anyone who stuck so much as a grain of that white shit up his nose on the actual *day* of his mother's funeral had to be some new and as yet undiscovered breed of sonofabitch. The lowest.

⑤
BaCK
TO
BaCK

"The thing I like about Harry Towns is that everything astonishes him."

An Italian writer friend he loved very much had been overheard making that remark and as far as Harry Towns was concerned it was the most attractive thing anyone had ever said about him. He wasn't sure it suited him exactly. Maybe it applied to the old him. But it did tickle him—the idea of a fellow past forty going around being astonished all the time. On occasion, he would use this description in conversation with friends. It did not slide neatly into the flow of talk. He had to shove it in, but he did, because he liked it so much. "Astonished" was probably too strong a word, but in truth, hardly a day passed that some turn of events did not catch him a little off guard. In football terms, it was called getting hit from the blind side. For example, one night, out of the blue, a girl he thought he knew pretty intimately came up with an extra marriage; she was clearly on record as having had one under her belt, but somehow the early union had slipped her mind. And for good measure, there was an eight-year-old kid in the picture, too, one who was stowed away somewhere in Maine with her first husband's parents. On another occasion, a long-time friend of Towns's showed up unannounced at his apartment with a twin brother, thin, pale, with a little less hair than Towns's buddy, and a vague hint of mental institutions around the eyes; but he was a twin brother, no question about it. So out of no-where, after ten years, there was not one but two Vinnys and Harry Towns was supposed to absorb the extra one and go about his business. Which he did, except that he had to be thrown a little off stride. It was that kind of thing. Little shockers, almost on a daily basis.

Late one night, the slender Eurasian woman who ran his favorite bar turned to the "gypsies," an absolute rock-bottom handful of stalwarts who closed the place regularly at four in the morning (and after eight years of working a "straight" job, nine-to-five, how he loved being one of them) and suddenly, erratically, screamed out, "You're all shits," flinging her cash register through the window. What kind of behavior was that? She was famed for handling difficult situations with subtlety and finesse. Towns tried to grab on to some gross piece of behavior that might have brought on this outburst—the only one of which she had been guilty in anyone's memory. All he could come up with was that one of them had slumped over and fallen asleep with his head on the table. A film dubber had done that, halfway through his dinner. Is that why they were all shits? What's so shitty about that?

If you walked the streets of the city, there was plenty to be astonished about. He supposed that was true if you lived in Taos, New Mexico, but he wasn't convinced of it. One day Towns saw an elderly and distinguished-looking man with homburg and cane hobble off briskly in pursuit of a lovely young girl. She was about twenty feet ahead of him and kept taking terrified looks over her shoulder at him. About that brisk hobbling. It's a tough one to pull off, but that's exactly what he was doing. She was stumbling along, not handling her high heels too well. Even though she was more or less running and he was doing his hobbling motion, the gap between them wasn't getting any wider. It was a crowded sunny lunchtime with plenty of secretaries floating around. Towns seemed to be the only one on the street who was aware of this rope of urgency between the man and the girl; he caught onto it, falling in step with them. The girl twirled through traffic, caught her heel in a manhole cover, and fell, long legs gaping, flowered skirt above her hips, black magnificent cunt screaming at the sky. The man stopped, leaning on his cane, as though he did not want to press his advantage. Towns stopped, too. She seemed to take an awfully long time getting herself together. Not that there was any studied sensuality to her behavior. The confusion appeared to come out of those early terrified looks over her shoulder. The girl was striking and even aristocratic-looking, that movie kind of Via Veneto aristocracy. Dominique Sanda, if you insist. But there was a young-colt brand of clumsiness in the picture, too. She started to run again and the man in the homburg resumed his inevitable

pursuit of her. The girl went through the revolving door
of a department store and, after a few beats, the man
followed her. That's when Towns decided to call it a day.
He could not testify to his source of information, but he
would have laid four to one they were going to wind up in
the lingerie department. They would get there by esca-
lator. What was Towns going to do up there with them?
What was he going to see? The manhole tableau was a
tough act to follow, so he decided to take it for what it
was, a perfect little erotic cameo that might just as well
have been staged for his benefit. It was a gift. He owned it
and could play it back any time he wanted to.

Now maybe events like that were a dime a dozen in
Taos, New Mexico. He doubted it. On the other hand, he
had never been there so he couldn't say.

If there were small daily shockers in his life, the broad
lines of Harry Towns's life had been clean and predict-
able. He had a good strong body and a feeling that it was
not going to let him down. Thus far, knock wood, it
hadn't. He had always sensed that he would have a son
and they would have baseball catches in a back yard
somewhere. He had the son and they had plenty of
catches. About ten years' worth. After a shaky start, he
realized he had the knack of making money, not the kind
that got you seaside palaces, but enough to keep everyone
comfortable. Which he did. Early on in his marriage, he
saw a separation coming; he wasn't sure when, but it was
coming all right, and it came. He had read somewhere
that when it came to the major decisions in life, all you
had to do was listen to the deep currents that ran inside
yourself, and they would tell you which way to go. He

listened to his and they told him to get going. His wife must have been tuned in to some currents of her own. So they split up and there wasn't much commotion to it. He gave them both a slightly above-average grade on the way they had handled it. After all, take a look at the reason they had gotten married. It dated back to a time when, if you slept with a girl, it meant you had somehow "damaged" her and were obligated to snap her up for a lifetime. He had never told that to anyone, including his wife, but under oath, he would have to identify that as the reason he had gone down the aisle with her. (And it was some sleeping. Exactly twice, in a Plymouth, or at least half in and half out of one, with a door open. During the second session, her father had run outside in a bathrobe and caught them at it. His way of handling his daughter's getting laid was to put his hands on his hips, stick out his jaw and say, "I see that position is everything in life.") Towns had to be fair. There was at least one other reason he had gotten married. She was pretty. She'd had a screen test. The first time he spotted her, it almost tore his head off. He wasn't sure *what* he was, and at the time he'd felt it was a little on the miraculous side that he'd been able to get such an attractive girl interested in him. So he felt he had better marry her, because there was no telling what was coming. It might be his last shot at a pretty girl. That had all been a long time ago. He liked cocaine now—let's face it, he had a modest habit going. On occasion, he had slept with two girls at a time and he had gotten to the point where he didn't think it was anything to raise the flag about. The first time, it was really something, but after that, it was just a matter of having an extra girl in there with you. Even if you had twelve to work with, all you could really concentrate on was one.

In any case, there had been some significant detours along the way, but you couldn't say, overall, that there had been any wild outrageous swerves to his life. Only when it came to his father did he get handed a script that was entirely different from the one he had had in mind.

For forty years, Towns's mother and father had lived in a once-pleasant section of the city that, to use the polite phrase, had "gone down." To get impolite about it, it meant that the Spanish and black people had moved in and the aging Jews, their sons and daughters long gone, had slipped off to "safer" sections of the city. Whether any of this was good or bad, and no matter how you sliced it, it was now a place where old people got hit over the head after dark. Young people did, too, but especially old people. Harry Towns's father had plenty of bounce to his walk and had been taking the subway to work for sixty years. Towns was fond of saying that his father was "seventy-five, going on fifty"; yet technically speaking, his parents were in the old department and he didn't want to get a call one day saying they had been hit over the head. Clearly, he wanted to get them out of there. It was just that he was a little slow in getting around to doing something about it. He sent them on a couple of minor-league vacations to Puerto Rico. He took them to at least one terrific restaurant a week and he phoned them all the time, partly to make sure they hadn't gotten killed. The one thing he didn't do was rent an apartment for them, get it furnished, lay out a year's rent or so, take them down to it, and say, "Here. Now you have to move in. And the only possible reason to go back to the old place is to get your clothes. And you don't even have to do that." He was in some heavy tax trouble and he was not exactly setting the world on fire in the money department, but he could have pulled it off. How about the cocaine he bought? A year's worth of it—right there—could have handled six months' rent for a terrific one-bedroom apartment on lower Park Avenue. Which is what his father, in particular, had his eye on. From that location, he would be able to take one of his bouncy walks right over to work and bid a fond farewell to the subway. But Towns didn't do any of this for his folks and it was a failure he was going to have to carry on his back for a long time.

One day, Towns's mother received a death sentence and it all became academic. She wasn't budging and forget about a tour of the Continent before she went under. Maybe Towns would take one when he got *his* verdict; she just wanted to sit in a chair in her own apartment and be left alone. It was going to be one of those slow wasting jobs. She would handle it all by herself and give the signal when it was time to go to the hospital and get it over with. As she got weaker—and with this disease, ironically, you became physically bigger—Towns's father got more snap to him. It wasn't one of those arrangements in which you could say, metaphorically, that her strength was flowing into him. Or that he was stealing it from her. It's just that he had never handled things better. He had probably never handled things at all. It got into areas like holding her hand a lot even in the very late stages when she had turned into some kind of sea monster and the hands had become great dried-out claws. (He had seen something like what she resembled at California's Marineland, an ancient seal that could hardly move. It wasn't even much of an attraction for people; it just sat there, scaled and ancient, and about all you could say about it was that it was alive.) When they took her false teeth out so she wouldn't be able to swallow them, it gave her mouth a broken-fencepost look, with a tooth here and a tooth there, but Towns's father kissed her snaggled lips as though she were a fresh young girl on her way to a dance. He just didn't see any monster lying there. Harry Towns did, but his father didn't. When he was a boy, Towns remembered his father wearing pullovers all the time. He had been a little chilly all his life. The hospital released Towns's mother for a short time. The radiation made her yearn for cold air, so Towns's dad laid there next to her all night with great blasts of bedroom air-conditioning showering out on the two of them. He offered her the soothing cold while his own bones froze. Towns didn't know it at the time, but he was going to remember all of this as being quite beautiful. Real romance, not your movie bullshit. And it hadn't been that kind of marriage. For forty-five years, they had cut each other to ribbons; they had done everything but fight a duel with pistols. Yet he led her gently into death, courtly, loving, never letting go of her hand, in some kind of old-fashioned way that Towns didn't recognize as going on anymore. Maybe it had gone on in the Gay Nineties or some early time like that.

And Towns's father kept getting bouncier. That was the only flaw in the setup. He probably should have been getting wan and gray, but he got all this extra bounce instead. He couldn't help it. That's just the way he got. The only time he ever left Towns's mother was to go down to work. He would bounce off in the morning looking nattier than ever. He was the only fellow in the world Towns thought of as being natty. Maybe George Raft was another one. Towns remembered a time his father had been on an air-raid-warden softball team and gone after a fly ball in center field. He slipped, fell on his back, got to his feet with his ass all covered with mud—but damned if he didn't look as natty as ever. In fact, there was only one unnatty thing Towns could remember his father ever doing. It was when he took his son to swimming pools and they both got undressed in public locker rooms and his father tucked his undershirt between his legs so Towns couldn't see his cock. The maneuver was probably designed to damp down the sexiness of the moment, but actually it worked the other way, the tucked-in undershirt looking weirdly feminine on a hairy-chested guy and probably turning Towns on a little. His father definitely did not look natty during those moments.

It was a shame the old man (an expression that never quite fit) had to leave Towns's sick mother to go down to work. There was a Spanish record shop across the street that played Latin rhythm tunes full blast all day long and into the night. There was no way to get it across to the owners that a woman was dying of cancer about fifty feet away and two stories up and could they please keep the volume down a little. In their view, they were probably livening up the neighborhood a bit, giving it a badly needed shot in the arm. Possibly, on their native island, they kept the music up all the time, even during cancer. On two separate occasions, the apartment was robbed, once when his mother had dozed off. The second time, she sat there and watched them come in through the fire-escape window. They took the television set and a radio. The way Towns got the story, she merely waved a weary sea claw at them as if to say, "Take anything you want. I've got cancer." Oddly enough, they never got to Towns's father's strongbox which was in a bedroom bureau drawer and not that difficult to find if you were in the least bit industrious. All his life, Towns had wondered about the

secrets that were in there; and also how much his father
made a week. The news of the robberies just rolled off the
shoulders of Towns's dad. It didn't take a bit of the bounce
out of him. He comforted Towns's mother with a hug and
then zipped inside to cook something she could get down.

A cynical interpretation of all this snap and bounciness
might have been that Towns's dad was looking ahead.
Towns was fond of saying his father had never been sick
a day in his life. Actually, it wasn't quite true. He had had
to spend a year strapped to a bench for his back and
Towns remembered a long period in which his dad was
involved with diathermy treatments. They didn't sound
too serious, but Towns was delighted when his father
could say good-bye to them. That was about the extent of
it. He had every one of his teeth and a smile that could
mow down entire crowds. Towns's dentist would stick an
elbow in his ribs and say, "How come you don't have teeth
like your dad's?" Tack on all that nattiness and bounce
and you had a pretty attractive guy on your hands. Maybe
he was just giving the old lady a handsome sendoff so he
could ease his conscience and clear the decks for a terrific
second-time-around. Was it possible he had someone
picked out already? For years, Towns's mother had been
worried about a certain buyer who had been with the firm
for years and "worked close" with Towns's dad. Except
that Towns didn't buy any of this. There were certain
kinds of behavior you couldn't fake. You couldn't hold that
claw for hours and kiss that broken mouth if you were
looking ahead. You could do other things, but you couldn't
do those two. At least he didn't think so. Besides, Towns
was doing a bit of looking ahead on his dad's behalf. He
had put himself in charge of that department. And that's
about all he was in charge of. He was almost doing a

great many things. He almost went down to the Spanish record shop and told them that they had better lower the music or he would break every record over their fucking heads. After the second robbery, he called a homicide detective friend and said he wanted to make a thorough cruise of the neighborhood and take a shot at nailing the guys who'd come up through the fire escape. He would go through every mug shot in the files to find the sonsofbitches. Except that he didn't. He came very close to getting his mother to switch doctors, using some friends to put him in touch with a great cancer specialist who might give her a wild shot at some extra life. He was Captain Almost. Over and over, he asked his father if he needed any money to which he would reply, "We've got plenty. You just take care of yourself." One day Towns said the hell with it and wrote out a check for two thousand dollars; this was money he really needed, although, in truth, a third of it would have gone over to coke. Mysteriously, he never got around to mailing it. There was only one department in which he demonstrated some follow-through. It's true he hadn't rented an apartment on lower Park Avenue for his parents and gotten them out of their old neighborhood, but that's a mistake he wasn't going to make again. He would wait a polite amount of time after his mother died and then he would make his move, set up the place, get his father down there to lower Park if he had to use a gun to get the job done. He sure as hell was getting at least one of them out. He would give up the coke for that. He would give up two fingers and a toe if he had to. He was going to put his father right there where he could bounce over to work and never have to ride a subway again. About ten blocks away from work would be perfect. Towns's father didn't want to retire.

That business place of his was like a club; his cronies were down there. And the crisp ten-block walk to work would keep that snap in his walk. There was more to the script that Towns had written. His father could take broads up there with him. That buyer, if he liked, or anyone else he felt like hanging out with. Someone around forty-seven would be just right for him. Towns would scoop up a certain girl he had in mind and maybe they would all go out together. He didn't see that this showed any disrespect for his mother. What did one thing have to do with the other? Once his father was in the city, they would spend more time together, not every night, but maybe twice a week and Sundays for breakfast. He had had his father out with some friends and some of them said he fit right in with them. It was nice of them to say that. And even if he did not exactly fit in, at least he didn't put into play any outrageous old-guy things that embarrassed everybody. They would just have to accept him once in a while whether he fit in or not. Otherwise he would get some new friends.

That was the general drift of the script he had written for his father. But the key to it was the apartment. Right after they buried his mother, Towns called a real-estate agent and told her to start hunting around in that general lower Park vicinity. He used the same agent who'd gotten him his own apartment. He read her as being in her late thirties and not bad. Nothing there for him but maybe for his father. Towns's dad and the agent would prowl around, checking out apartments, and maybe get something going. He didn't have the faintest idea if his father's guns were still functional in that area, but he preferred to think they were. Maybe he would ask him. So Towns set the apartment hunt in motion and, after a few weeks, took his father to dinner at a steak house and hit him with it. "Let's face it, fun is fun, but you've got to get out of there, Dad."

"I know, Harry, and I will, believe me, but I just don't feel like it right now. I have to feel like it. Then I will." At that moment, Harry Towns noticed that his father had lost a little weight, perhaps a few more pounds than he had any business losing. He was one of those fellows who had been one weight all his adult life—and now he was a different one.

"I don't have any appetite," he said.

"But look how you're eating now," Towns told him. And, indeed, his father had cleaned up everything in front of him. Then Towns gave his father a small lecture. "Let's face it, Dad, you're a little depressed. You can't live with somebody that long and then lose them and not be. Maybe you ought to see somebody, for just an hour or two. I had that experience myself. Just one or two sessions and I got right back on the track." He didn't want to use the word "psychiatrist." But that's what he had in mind. He knew just the right fellow, too. Easy on the nerves and almost the same age as his father. He had expected to hear some grumbling, but his father surprised him by saying, "Maybe you have a point there." And then Towns's dad looked at him with some kind of wateriness in his eyes. It wasn't tears, or even the start of them, but some kind of deep and ancient watery comprehension. Then he cleaned off his plate and brought up the subject of bank books and insurance. Towns felt he was finally getting in on some of the secrets in the strongbox. He had about fifty grand in all and he wanted his son to know about it, "just in case anything happens."

"There ain't anything gonna happen," said Towns.

"Just in case. I want it split fifty-fifty, half for you and half for your brother."

"Give it all to him," said Towns.

"Never," said his father, with something close to anger. "Half and half, right down the middle. And it's nothing to sneeze at."

"I know that."

"I thought you were making fun of it."

"I wasn't," said Towns. "But will you get the goddamn apartment?"

"I will," he said, mopping up the last of the cheesecake. "But first I have to feel like it."

The appetite thing worried Towns. He was sure it connected to some kind of depression, because he ate so well when he was out with Towns. But he couldn't have breakfast with his father every morning. And no matter how much he loved him, he couldn't eat with him every goddamn night. What about lunches? Was he supposed to run over and have lunch with him, too? He finally teamed the old man up with the real-estate lady, and on a Saturday morning they checked out a few available apartments. On lower Park. That afternoon, the woman called Towns and said his father had gotten dizzy in one of the apartments and hit his head on the radiator. She said she had made him swear he was in good shape before she let him go home. She was all right. Towns got his father to go to the doctor—he admitted to getting dizzy once before on the subway and having to ask someone for a seat—and they ran some tests. They used the same doctor who hadn't performed any particular miracles on his mother's claws. Towns had meant to switch off to another one, but that's something else he had not gotten around to. The tests zeroed in on his prostate and Towns felt better immediately. He had a little condition of his own and he knew it was no toothache, but there was no way it could turn you into a Marineland exhibition. The prostate had to go and the fellow who would take it out was named Doctor Merder. Towns and his dad had a good laugh about that one. If you were a surgeon with a name like that, you had better be good. So they didn't worry a bit about him. The book on the doctor was that he had never lost a prostate case. Towns's dad checked into the hospital. He was concerned about how the business, or "place" as he called it, would run in his absence and he didn't relax until the boss called and told him to take it easy, they would cover for him and everything would be just fine; just relax and get better. The boss was around thirty years younger than he was, but Towns's dad couldn't get over his taking the time to do a thing like that. Once in the hospital, he went from natty to dignified. Maybe he had always been dignified, even though he had blown his one shot at being head of his own business, years before. Using some fancy accounting techniques, his partners had quickly cut him to ribbons and eased him out of his share of the firm. This would have left most men for dead; but Towns's dad had simply gone back to his old factory job as second in command, dignified as ever. In the hospital, the only thing he used the bed for was sleeping. He sat in a flowered New England chair, neat as a pin, reading the books Harry Towns brought him. His favorite kind of book dealt with generals and statesmen, people like Stettinius and Franklin Delano Roosevelt, and the goings-on behind the scenes during World War II. Or at least Towns assumed they were his favorites. Maybe they were his own favorites, and all those years he had been pushing them on his dad. Whenever Towns brought him a book, his father felt obliged to "read it up," as if it would be "wasted" if he didn't. Like food. So whenever Towns showed up at the hospital with another one, he would hold up his hands and say, "Stop, for crissakes. How much can a guy read?"

Along with at least one volume about Secret-Service shenanigans in World War II, Towns would also bring a fistful of expensive Canary Island cigars. For most of his life, his father had smoked a cheaper brand, Admiration Joys when Towns was a boy, but in recent years Towns had promoted him to these higher-priced jobs. He complained that Towns was spoiling him. Sixty cents was too much to spend for a cigar. And there was no way to go back to the Joys. But he got a lot of pleasure out of the expensive ones. Towns had gotten the cigar habit from his father; he remembered a time when his father would greet a friend by stuffing a cigar in his handkerchief pocket and the friend would do the same for Towns's dad. It seemed like a fine ritual and Towns was sorry to see it go; there was probably a paper around proving it was all very phallic and homosexual. Now, when Towns showed up with the cigars, his father would say, "What the hell am I supposed to do with them?"

"Smoke 'em," said Towns.

"What if I don't feel like it?"

"Then just take a few puffs."

"All right, leave 'em over there."

And he would. He would take a few puffs of each one. So they wouldn't go to waste.

They kept taking more tests on Towns's dad; he didn't leave the room very often, but he did spend a little time with one other patient and he got a tremendous kick out of this fellow. He was trying to impeach the President and Towns's father couldn't get over that. If he had great admiration for people like Cordell Hull and Omar Bradley, his respect for the office of the President was absolutely overpowering. The idea of a guy running around trying to get the top executive impeached tickled the hell out of Towns's dad. It was so outrageous. "You got to see this guy," he told Towns. "He's got a sign this big over his door, some kind of impeachment map. He's trying to get some signatures up. And he's important, too. I don't know what the hell he does, but he gives off an important impression. He says he wants to meet you."

"What's he want to meet me for?"

"I don't know. Maybe he heard you were important, too. Why don't you go over there and give him a tumble?"

Towns wasn't terribly interested in the impeachment man. He was more interested in the tests. But for his father's sake, he met the fellow in the lounge. He was a sparse-haired gentleman, a bit younger than his father, who talked a mile a minute and seemed to be carefully staying off the subject of impeachment. At the same time, he kept checking Towns's eyes as if he were looking for a go-ahead signal. Towns gave him a signal that said nothing doing. "What'd you think of him?" Towns's father asked as they walked back to the room.

"He's all right," said Towns.

"Well, I don't know what *you* think of him, but to me he's really something. Imagine a thing like that. Going around trying to im*peach* the President of the United States. And he's no bum. You can tell that by looking at him. I think he's got some dough." All the way back to his room, Towns's dad kept clucking his tongue about the fellow. He acted as though it was the most amazing thing he had ever come across in all his seventy-five years.

"Would you like to see that map he's got on the outside of his door?"

"I don't think so, Dad."

"I think you ought to take a look at it."

"Maybe I will, on the way out."

They decided to build up Towns's dad by giving him a couple of transfusions before the surgery. While this was going on, Towns ran into a nurse who came an inch short of being one of the prettiest girls he knew in the city. He had always meant to get around to her, but she lived with a friend of his and he claimed that was one rule he would never break. Or at least he'd try not to break it. She had a private patient down the hall and said she knew about his father and that a week before, he had stood outside his door and asked her to come in and have a cookie. Towns wished his father had been much more rascally than that. Why didn't he just reach out and pinch her ass? On the other hand, the cookie invitation wasn't much, but it was something. Towns made her promise to go in and visit him and sort of kid around with him and she said of course she would, he didn't even have to ask. He had the feeling this was the kind of girl his father would love to fool around with in an old-guy way.

The transfusion gave Towns's father some fever, but they went ahead and operated anyway. This puzzled Towns a bit. Except that his father seemed to come out of the surgery all right. He didn't appear to be connected up to that many tubes, which struck Towns as a good sign. Towns kept bringing him books about desert warfare, the defense of Stalingrad, Operation Sea Lion, but he kept them over to the side where his father couldn't see them and have to worry about "reading them up." Before they got spoiled. On the third day after the operation, he brought along a real torpedo of a cigar, long, fragrant, aromatic, the best he could find.

"What'd you bring that for?" asked his father, who was down to one tube.

"Why do you think?"

"I ain't smoking it, Harry."

"The hell you're not."

The next day, his father looked a little weaker, but the doctor said it was more or less normal to take a dip on the way back from surgery. When they were alone, Towns's father asked his son, "What the hell are you doing here?"

"I came to see you, Dad."

He turned his head away, waved his hand in disgust and said, "You ain't gonna do me any good." Then he turned back and chuckled and they started to talk about what was going on outside, but that cruel random slash had been there. Maybe you were allowed to be a little cruel right after surgery. Towns wasn't sure. It was only the second piece of bad behavior Towns could think of since he'd been born. The other had to do with Towns at around eight or nine, using the word "schmuck" about somebody; he didn't know what the word meant, but his father instantly lashed out and belted him halfway across the city. So that added up to two in more than forty years. "Schmuck" and "You ain't gonna do me any good." Not a bad score. The next morning, the doctor phoned and told Towns he had better come down, because his father's pulse had stopped. "What do you mean, stopped?" Towns asked.

"The nurse stepped out for a second and when she came back he had no pulse. She called a round-the-clock resuscitation team and they were down there like Johnny-on-the-spot. They do quite a job."

"How come the nurse stepped out?"

"They have to go to the bathroom."

"Is he gonna live?"

"It depends on how long his pulse stopped. We'll know that later."

Towns got down there fast. He met the doctor in the intensive-care unit. The doctor asked if he would like to see the team working on his dad and he said he would. He took Towns down the hall and displayed the huge resuscitation units the way a proud Soviet manager would show off his plant for a group of Chrysler execs. His father was hooked up to plenty of tubes now. He was like a part in a huge industrial city. The whole city of Pittsburgh. He was the part that took a jolting spasmodic leap every few seconds. Towns got as close as he could—what the hell, he'd seen everything now. He tried to spot something that wasn't covered up by gadgets. Something that looked like his father. He finally picked off a section from the wrist to the elbow that he recognized as being his father's arm. He was pretty sure of it. "There's no point in your staying around," the doctor said. "I know that," said Towns.

He went up to his father's room and got the cigar. Then he walked to the end of the hall and took a look at the impeachment map. It showed how much strength the fellow had across the country. He didn't have much. A couple of pins in Los Angeles, Wisconsin, New York, and out. On the way down, Towns stopped in at the snack bar and had some peach yogurt. It was the first time in his life he had ever tasted yogurt and it wasn't bad. It went down easy and it didn't taste the way he had imagined it would. He made a note to pick up a few cartons of it. The fruit kind. He went back to his apartment and fell asleep. The call came early in the evening. Towns had promised himself he would fix the exact time in his mind forever, but a week later, he couldn't tell you what time or even what month it had happened.

"That's it, huh?"

"I'm afraid so," said the doctor. "About five minutes ago. I'd like to get your permission to do a medical examination of dad so that maybe we can find out something to help the next guy who comes in with the same condition."

"How come you operated on him with fever?"

"We tried to contact you on that to get your permission."

"You should've tried harder."

"See," said the doctor, "that's just it. We talk to people when they're understandably upset and they say no to medical examinations. In Sweden, it's automatic."

"Work a little harder on what you know already."

"The next one could be your child. Or your children's children."

"Fuck you, doctor."

So that was it. The both of them. And for the moment, all Harry Towns had out of it was a new expression. Back to back. He had lost both his parents, back to back. He leaned on that one for about six months or so; especially if someone asked him why he was "low" or why he was late on a deadline. "Hey," he would say, "I lost both my parents, back to back." And he would be off the hook. He told his brother from Omaha to fly in as fast as possible and take care of everything, clean out his dad's apartment, settle the accounts, the works. He was better at that kind of thing. Maybe Towns would be good at it, too, but he didn't want to be. The only thing he could hardly wait to do was get in touch with the rabbi who had officiated over his mother's funeral. He was a fellow the chapel kept on tap in case you didn't have any particular rabbi of your own in mind. It was like getting an attorney from Legal Aid except that this one turned out to be a real find. He showed up in what Harry Towns liked to recall as a cloud of smoke, with a shiny black suit and a metaphysical tuft of hair sticking up on his head. He turned up two and a half minutes before the ceremony and asked Towns to sum up his mother. "What are you, nuts?" said Towns. "Trust me," said the rabbi, a homely fellow with an amazingly rocklike jaw that was totally out of sync with his otherwise wan Talmudic features. Towns took a shot. He told him they really shouldn't have limos taking his mother out to the grave, they ought to have New York taxis. Whenever she had a problem, she would simply jump inside one and have the driver ride around with the meter going while she talked to him until she felt better. Then she would pay the bill, slap on a big tip, and hop out. That was her kind of psychoanalysis. She couldn't cook and Towns didn't want anyone laying that word "housewife" on her. Not at the funeral. It was very important to get her right. This was almost as important to him as losing her. She was close to cabbies, bellhops, and busboys and she could brighten up a room just by walking into it. And damned if this faded little mysterious house rabbi didn't get her. In two and a half minutes. "Sparkle" was the key word. And it was his own. He kept shooting that word "sparkle" out over the mourners and it was as if he had known her all his life. Towns had never seen a performance quite like that.

After they had buried her in the Jersey Flats, the rabbi asked if anyone could give him a lift back to New York

City. Everyone was staying at an aunt's house in Jersey, so no one could. With that, he hopped on the hearse. And then he disappeared; once again, it might just as well have been in a cloud of smoke. And he was only seventy-five bucks. So you can see why Towns was anxious to have him back for a repeat performance. It was enough to get Towns back to religion. Why not, if they had unsung guys like that around? Except that the minute he showed up at the chapel the second time, something was a little off. The rabbi looked barbered for one thing. And he was wearing flowing rabbinical robes. What happened to the black shiny suit that he had probably brought over from Poland? And he didn't get Towns's father at all. "Good, honest, hard-working man." "Lived only for his family." Shit like that. Right out of your basic funeral textbook. The very thing Towns wanted to head off. His diction was different, fancier. He could have been talking about anybody. And he seemed to be playing not to the audience but strictly to Towns. It occurred to Harry Towns that maybe there wasn't any way to get his father. Maybe that was it—honest, hard-working, et cetera. But for Christ's sake, he could have found something. "Sparkle" wasn't it—he had used that anyway—but how about that bounce in his walk. What about nattiness for a theme. The sharpness of his beard against Harry Towns's face when he was a kid. Anything. Cigar smoking. Handing them out and getting some back. His being an air-raid warden. An all-day fist fight he had with his brother. (When it was over, they didn't talk to each other for twenty-five years.) Anything at all. Just so they didn't bury a statistic. Maybe it was as simple as the old second-audition syndrome. A performer would come in and knock you on your ass the first time. He would get called back and bomb. Show people explained it by saying there was nothing on the line the first time a performer auditioned. If you called him back, it meant you were considering him for the part. In that situation, nine out of ten performers choked. The rabbi didn't choke. He was as smooth as silk. He probably felt he was really cooking. But he sure did bomb.

Out they went to the Jersey Flats again, and after his father was in the ground, alongside his mother, the rabbi took Towns aside and said, "With your mother, I didn't even know who you were." Who in the hell was he? A screenwriter? So that was it. The rabbi had caught his name on a picture and felt he had to be classier. "I'm being sponsored on a little trip to Israel," said the rabbi. "Is there any chance you could meet me there so we could see it together? It would be meaningful to both of us."

"I don't give a shit about Israel," said Towns. It wasn't true. He did give a shit about Israel. When the chips were down, he was still some kind of Jew. He was just sore as hell at the rabbi for letting him down and not getting his father right. And for not being that magical fellow with the tuft of hair who had shown up in a cloud of smoke and almost got him back to religion. After everyone had climbed back into the limos, Towns went back to the grave and dropped that big torpedo of a cigar inside. He was aware of the crummy sentimentality involved—and he knew he would probably tell it to a friend or two before the week was over—as an anecdote—but he did it anyway. No one was going to tell him whether to be sentimental or not—not when he had just lost his mother and father. Back to back.

He hung around the city while his brother cleaned things up for him. He said he didn't want anything from the apartment except an old-fashioned vest-pocket watch he remembered. And maybe his dad's ring, with the initials rubbed over with age so you couldn't really make them out. They got the finances straightened out in his brother's hotel room. The money coming to Towns was enough to cover his back tax bill to the government, almost to the penny. He hadn't slept easily for a year, wondering where he was going to get that kind of dough. And there were a handful of salary checks to be divided up. So he finally found out what his father's salary was. It was probably the last secret in the strongbox. He was sorry he found out. They had cut him down to nickels and dimes, probably because he was seventy-five. And here he was, settling his son's tax bill. Towns hugged his brother, saying, "Let's stay in touch. You're all I've got," and then his nephew came dancing out in one of his father's suits. Wearing a funny smile and looking very natty. Towns recalled a fellow he had once worked for who had come to the office wearing his father's best suit, one day after the old man had died. At the time, he wondered, what kind of a guy does that. Now, his brother said, "It fit him like a glove, so why not?" Towns couldn't answer that one. He just felt it shouldn't be going on. About a month later, he changed his mind and was glad the kid took the clothes.

Harry Towns planned on taking a long drive to someplace he hadn't been so he could be alone and sort things out, but he got whisked off to California on a job he felt he couldn't turn down. He told himself the work would be good for him. Just before he left, he ran into the cookie nurse at a singles place and asked her if she had ever gone in and fooled around with his father. She said she had but her eyes told him she hadn't. Cunt. No wonder he hadn't moved in on her. It wasn't that she was living with his friend. The guy wasn't that close a friend. It was this kind of behavior. She would tell you that she would go in and screw around with your father and then she wouldn't.

He polished off the California work in about a week; whenever it sagged a little, he would say, "Hey, listen, I just lost both my parents, back to back." It burned him up when people advanced the theory that his father died because he couldn't live without his wife. He heard a lot of that and he didn't buy any of it. Towns hadn't been married to anyone for fifty years the way his father had and it didn't look as if there was going to be time to squeeze someone in for half a century. But he just couldn't afford to think that if you loved someone very much and they died, you had to hop right into the grave with them. He preferred to think that you mourned for them and then went about your business.

He went on an erratic crying schedule. The first burst came at the Los Angeles airport, on the way for a quick stopover in Vegas. He was really smoking with the late-night check-in stewardess at the L. A. airport, a small girl with a huge chest and an angel's face. He almost had her talked into going to Vegas with him. One extra shove and she would have been on the seat next to him. He did it right in front of the Air West pilots, too, and they didn't appreciate it much. On the other hand, two hookers saw the whole thing and got a big kick out of it. Then he got on the plane and cried all the way to Caesar's Palace. The hookers saw that one, too, and must have wondered if he were crazy. He had just finished hustling a stewardess. He might just as well have been Cary Grant back there at the airport. What was he doing all that crying for? Back East, he gave himself the job of copying over his address book. Halfway along, he came to his father's name and business number. He really went that time. For a period there, he didn't think he was ever going to stop. It was having to make that particular decision. What do you do, carry your dead father over into the new address book? Or drop him from the rolls, no more father, no more phone number, and you pick up that extra space for some new piece of ass?

He never did get to take that drive. The one in which he was going to go to a strange place and sort things out. The awful part is that he never seemed to get any huge lessons out of the things that happened to him. He was brimming over with small nuggets of information he had gathered for his work. For example, when frisking a homicide suspect in a stabbing case, the first thing detectives check for is a dry-cleaning ticket. On the theory that the suspect is going to ship his bloodstained clothing right off to the cleaner's. When shot at, cops are taught to jump to their left since most gunmen are right-handed and will either fire wide of the mark or, at worst, nick your shoulder. He knew there was no such thing as a second wind in running. If you got one, it meant you had not been "red-lining it," that is, running full out. He kept his young son enthralled for hours with this kind of information. But he didn't own any real wisdom and this bothered him. Instead, he borrowed other people's. Never sleep with a woman who has more problems than you do. Nelson Algren. Don't look over your shoulder because someone might be gaining on you. Satchel Paige. People behave well only because they lack the character to behave poorly. La Rochefoucauld. Take short views, hope for the best, and trust in God. Some British guy. Stuff like that. Wasn't it time for him to be coming up with a few of his own? Pressed to the wall, he would probably produce this list:

> *1. Be very lucky.*
> *2. Watch your ass.*

Because if they could get your father's pulse to stop—considering the way he looked, the way he bounced along, his smile, and the fifteen years, minimum, that Harry Towns had scripted up for him—if they could keep him out of that paid-for apartment on lower Park, and on top of everything, get him to die back to back with Towns's mom, the two of them stowed underground in the Jersey Flats, why then all bets were off and anything was possible. Anything you could dream up. You name it. Any fucking thing in the world.

6
anoTHer
Try

They weren't married. They weren't officially separated. They weren't much of anything. The way it worked is that each Sunday, Harry Towns's boy would be shipped into the city with a package of bills and Towns would take care of them; he saw it not so much in terms of paying them as whittling down the stacks as they arrived. At the time they broke up, he owned a massive wardrobe, mostly because he rarely threw away clothing and still had sweat shirts that dated twenty years back, ones he had bought at college. He left most of his clothing behind, although, admittedly, he took along his key outfits, four leather sport jackets and four pairs of his top slacks, in combinations that he could keep switching around so that he came across as being well dressed. A dapper newscaster who

had never been seen twice in the same outfit stopped
Harry Towns on several occasions and said, "Jesus, where
do you get your stuff?," a tribute to Towns's nimble foot-
work as a switcher of outfits. And a girl who worked in
costume design once said to him, "I understand you're not
afraid of clothing." He left his tax records behind, along
with his Army uniform and a ton of books; in this latter
category, he skimmed off the cream, fifty winners—books
like *Henry Esmond* and *Middlemarch,* ones he had read
but wanted to take a second and more mature shot at. He
left several suitcases with his wife, taking with him one
that was expensive and also professionally battered; it
was that way when he bought it and might have belonged
to an Italian film director, one whose career had been
uneven. The suitcase looked fine, but it weighed a ton—
before you put anything into it. He had always had a lot of
trouble picking out just the right suitcase; he knew, almost the second he bought this one, that it would soon be
on its way out. He left with what he saw as a lean and
mean assortment of items, and as far as he knew, his wife
had not thrown out the rest of his possessions. They met
for dinner once in a while, and if she had unloaded his old
sweat shirts, he felt he would have sensed it—but he
never asked her. He had gone to see a divorce lawyer
once, and they wound up talking about Ethel Merman.
And he had received a vague exploratory call from a
lawyer of hers. It stayed vague and finally petered out.
None of this added up to much of an arrangement, except
that built into it—and the reason they probably kept it
going that way—was the unspoken notion that at one
point or another they would give it Another Try. It was a
possibility that kept floating around on the edge of his
life; Towns liked to think it was the morning he woke up

and heard about the Tom Eagleton Vice-Presidential nomination that he decided to make his move.

To spell it out accurately, he did not wake up. It was ten in the morning, and he had never been asleep. He heard about Eagleton at a time when he was not only wide but outrageously awake, staring at the ceiling and flailing out for sleep as though it were a fish he had a chance of holding if he could just grab it. Inside his chest, an involuntary muscle snapped away like a tiny whip. This took place a little too far over to the left to be a heart attack, so he decided for the moment to sweep that possibility under the rug, though there was no way to rule it out entirely. It might have been fascinating to lie there and watch this snapping phenomenon take place in his own body, except that, at the moment, Harry Towns was in no mood to be fascinated. He had gotten himself into this by-now familiar condition by violating a basic cocaine rule: if you have any thought of falling asleep at night or accomplishing something when the sun comes up, you don't get under way by inhaling great vacuuming blasts of the drug at four in the morning. Which is what he had done. And in the past several months, he had piled up a dangerous number of violations. What happened is that for each transgression, in addition to the snapping, you lost an entire day. This was fine if you were a failed romantic poet and were supposed to touch bottom a few times, knock off a couple of sonnets, and check out at age thirty-three. But Harry Towns was a screenwriter in his forties, and each of those lost snapper days made it that much tougher to whittle down the pile of bills his son carried in on the train each Sunday. He knew that if he got up on one elbow, he could see a mound of them piled high on an end table. So he stayed as flat as he could.

The only reason he switched on the news was so he could tell himself he hadn't wasted the whole day. It was a little like nourishment. He would take some news into his system. This would enrich him and make him a slightly better person. And you never knew. A stray item about a union dispute or India's parliament might feed its way into a screenplay one day. So Harry Towns told himself he wasn't really staring at the ceiling, flailing out for sleep. An entire day was not being thrown over to lying around being shaky. He was working, soaking up information, doing a little research for future projects. It was bullshit, but it was all he had.

The actual sound of the news was not soothing to him. Music would have been better, even experimental-rock sounds. Best of all would have been a tomblike silence. Instead he had the crackle of the news and the traffic outside; even though he was thirty stories up, each car seemed to be headed into his mouth. It wasn't that difficult to see why Towns made the connection between himself and Eagleton. He and the Senator were the same age. And he came from a state in the Midwest right next to the one in which Towns had gone to college. They were in the same football conference. Eagleton was a family man, just like Towns, except that Eagleton had kept his family together, while Towns had let his own fall to pieces. He had that great name: Eagleton. It sounded just like the country. If America hadn't been named America, it could have been called Eagleton, and no one would have known the difference. Russia would never fool around with Eagleton, the Number One power. *If you don't like Eagleton, leave it!* So Harry Towns identified with this terrific new fellow who turned up out of nowhere and was going to get a try at the Vice-Presidency.

Towns loved people who came out of nowhere. In the one speech he had ever made, he told a group of high-school students that America was good because it kept coming up with people like that. The country had an endless supply. They came galloping out of nowhere just when you needed them. This was probably true about Finland, too, but Harry Towns didn't say that in his speech. Usually, you found out these "new" people had spent years building a foundation. A bit later, when Harry Towns got a look at the *New York Times* background profile, he found out that Eagleton was no exception.

He slipped out of the lobby of his apartment building to get the newspaper, looking around to make sure that a normal and pretty girl who lived up the street in a brownstone wasn't out walking her dog. They had flirted around a bit, and in a display of the new female consciousness elevation, she had reached out and pinched his ass in broad daylight. A very pretty girl had done that to him. He did not see himself as having set the world on fire, but wouldn't it be something if it turned out that he had gotten as far as he had because he had a cute ass? And only now were women allowed to let him know about it? That would be some shocker. Harry Towns felt strongly that the fallout from the move that women had made was terrific. For everybody. Or at least it was going to be. A statement he liked to throw out was: "I'm just sitting on the sidelines, waiting for the dust to settle." In actuality, he wasn't sitting on the sidelines. For example, he could now say to a woman, "Listen, I'm not an easy lay." The remark tended to back most of them off a bit, but some wound up enjoying it. This particular girl let him neck with her as long as they did it in the lobby of his building and she got to keep one hand on the mailbox and an eye on the street. As far as getting her up to his apartment, it was no dice. There was something charming about this arrangement, and Harry Towns meant to get around to her one day. This would be at some future point, after he had closed down his involvement with hookers and cocktail waitresses, freeing himself for everyday girls. Meanwhile, he didn't want to blow it by letting her see him after a cocaine night, his eyes filmed over and tufts of what was left of his hair shooting out in different directions. Before going out in the evening, he could get his hair to look fairly civilized by shampooing it a certain way and unloading half an aerosol can of thick hair spray on it. The only way to get away with his kind of weirdly tufted hair, *au naturel,* was to be an atomic physicist, which he wasn't, or to say the hell with it, this is me, which he couldn't. The normal girl was nowhere in sight, so he slipped across the street and bought a quart of Light 'n' Lively milk and the *Times*, both of which he took back to what he still referred to, only sardonically now, as his tower of steel and glass, high above Manhattan. One plus item in the cocaine column, in fact the only one he could think of at the moment, was that it deadened your appetite and kept you on the skinny side. That made it the world's most expensive diet. He could get the Light 'n' Lively down, but it would be midnight before he felt the first stirrings of appetite. He would probably want a couple of egg rolls then. Meanwhile, he sipped the milk and read the *Times*, gliding by the latest developments in SALT and zeroing in on the background Eagleton coverage. He just wasn't up to SALT breakthroughs at the moment. If he had been in love with Eagleton before, he was head over heels after he took a look at the fellow's picture. He looked exactly like his name. Towns loved his profile, and he loved his hairline. He had every one of his hairs and every one was in place. Towns felt that Eagleton deserved that hairline, too, after the way he had worked his way up, doing various jobs in the county, any one they threw at him, always performing selflessly and not getting caught in municipal-bond scandals. Just as Towns had suspected, he hadn't really come out of nowhere. They had a picture of his family in there, the one he had made sure to hold together, and they looked terrific, too. Towns had a famous racketeer friend who looked him in the eye one night and said he never trusted a man unless the fellow had "a tight family." He had his head blown off in a Queens restaurant, but Towns always remembered the remark and felt guilty about not having one himself.

The reason Harry Towns was so involved with the Vice-Presidential candidate was that, even though they were the same age and had gone to schools that were in the same football conference, Eagleton's life, a slow upward climb, was just coming into blossom, whereas Harry Towns saw himself as being on a downhill slide. Forget about his *seeing* himself on one. He really *was* on one. He could not even pass himself off as a fellow who had peaked. If he had, he wished someone had tapped him on the shoulder when he was way up on that peak so he could have taken out a little time to enjoy it. Tom Eagleton wasn't into coke. He sure as hell wasn't shelling out three hundred dollars a week for a quarter of an ounce and slowly easing his way into the half-ounce league; with money that should have been used to whittle down the huge stack of bills on the end table, money he could have turned over to his wife so she could buy a couch and some ottomans and have a complete living room like other people. Was Eagleton seeing his kid once a week, taking him to a monster movie, a Mexican restaurant, and then back to the train? Not on your life. Let's say that perfect family portrait in the *Times* was a little exaggerated for political purposes and that if you peeled off a layer or two there were a couple of serious problems in the Eagleton family, the kind everybody had. A heart murmur, something like that. At least Eagleton had hung in there and stuck around, so that no matter how badly he felt, his children could see him before they went to bed at night. He wasn't stretched out in any king-sized bed that had been recommended by *Playboy* magazine, watching a chest muscle snap. And finding traces of the hooker he had had up there with him the night before. (Harry Towns had been lucky with this particular hooker. She was a fresh young one, new on the street, and she didn't have a price list. She didn't say, "Turn over? Are you kidding! That's an extra ten." And when he unpeeled her, he had gotten a delightful surprise—long pretty legs, a perfect ass, and the name "Tony" tattooed above one nipple. She apologized for the Tony inscription, saying, "It took six bikers to hold me down and do it." That's all Towns had to hear. He tore into her and the tattoo, and unless she was the world's greatest actress, he got to her. There was a line around the block of ones he hadn't gotten to, so he felt qualified to know when he had struck paydirt.) None of which altered the fact that Eagleton wasn't spending his time in beds recommended by *Playboy* magazine, rolling around with tattooed hookers. He wasn't losing entire days sipping Light 'n' Lively, feeling shaky and looking ahead to the high point of his day, a lonely midnight egg roll. You didn't make that firm, steady climb to the nation's second biggest job with that type of behavior. So then the shock-treatment story broke, and under other circumstances, Harry Towns might have permitted himself an ironic chuckle. Except that he was in no condition to do any ironic chuckling. Besides, Towns looked at it this way: even while Eagleton was soaking up shock treatments, the man wasn't busy busting up any families. He probably had a lot of life insurance and wasn't forking over any three hundred dollars a week to coke dealers. He did his work, electrodes or no electrodes. A few blasts and right back to the desk. With no time for tattooed hookers. Unless that was the next big story on the horizon. Even if it was, it had nothing to do with Harry Towns.

He had been carrying around that notion of Another Try long before he had heard of Tom Eagleton. He didn't like the quality of his life, and he saw his wife and his old family as a means of protecting him from it. For example, he knew how to get a silencer. Now where did he come off knowing how to get one of those? It was easy to get a gun in the city, but a silencer was another story. A bartender showed him one and said that any time he needed one like it, he could have it for him in twenty-four hours. They came from Jersey. Why did Harry Towns have to know how to get something like that? From sunup to sundown, he had once played baseball in the shadow of a great stadium and dreamed of becoming a serious man. *Coriolanus* was his favorite play, and now he knew how to get a silencer. One friend was a homicide detective who would drop around to Towns's place without calling and tell him how depressing it was to work with dead bodies all the time. The detective said his best friend was the *Te Amo* cigar, which neutralized the smell of corpses; he was never without a pocketful. So Towns knew this about *Te*

Amo cigars. Because this was the type of friend he had, the kind of fellow who just dropped by. Towns was fairly relaxed in his apartment, but never one hundred percent, because at any moment, some dangerous person might walk in on him. He knew a fellow with the face of a French mime who stopped pimp cars, flashing a fake badge and a real pistol, then shook down the drivers for entire kilos of cocaine. He would show up in a bar Towns went to, his hands shaking, his heart virtually jumping out of his chest, saying, "I just did it. Come into the john and I'll show you what I got." He wouldn't give Towns any of the cocaine, just show him giant balls of it in glassine wrappers and then stick out his hands and say, "Look how shaky they are." The fellow said he wanted to get in a lot of this type of activity, because in six months he was "going up." It seemed a peculiar way to while away the days before you went to prison. It would have seemed more intelligent to maintain a low profile or to spend some time in self-improvement. For example, by taking a language course. Towns wondered about the prison fags and the possibility of being turned into one, to which the wild fellow with the French mime's face said, "I *do* take a lot of head."

In the shadow of that great stadium, most of Towns's friends were slated for careers in heart medicine, or at least orthodontia. Some had gotten Bausch & Lomb scholarships, and Towns himself had finished high school with a ninety-three average. Now he knew people who were "going up"; bodyguards and fellows who owned hidden pieces of hotels, one of them holding secret title to the twenty-eighth floor of a famed Miami one. He could understand the charm of knowing a few people like this, but not having them become your entire crowd. A girl he knew had been taken to Pennsylvania, sprinkled with cleaning fluid, and lit up. And Harry Towns had slept with her. Found her in a bar, took her home, screwed her matter-of-factly for about an hour and a half, took her back to the bar, where they both went about their business. The decision to keep it casual and matter-of-fact was hers, as well as his. And then she had been set on fire. He had once had his cock in this girl who got burned to a crisp. It had something to do with a kickback on an engineering contract. This gives you an idea of Harry Towns's circle. Another friend was a pimp who showed him two hundred twenty thousand dollars in a pair of shoes. But he didn't offer Towns any. He would turn up in a rented car, carrying a fortune in recording equipment, and play Harry Towns pimping tunes he had written. He wanted to make a switch from pimping into songwriting, and had the idea Towns could smooth this transition. He was a nice enough fellow, but he was also one more of a certain type of friend Towns had. Towns wound up getting him some coke, fixing him up with a waitress, and saying to himself, "Hey, wait a minute, who's the pimp around here?" It's possible that's what made the fellow such a topflight pimp. Because he could get people like Towns to do such things for him.

An attorney he respected scared the hell out of Harry Towns by saying, rather onimously, "You're getting a little close to the fire." On the positive side of the ledger, he was friendly with an all-pro defensive linebacker for the National Football League. But examine the circumstances in which they had met. The fellow had walked into one of Harry Towns's bars with a big grin on his face, put an arm around him, and said he wanted to buy them both a drink because he had just received his initiation into back-door sex. In the course of being blown by an Australian hooker, he had let drop the fact that he was an all-pro defensive linebacker for the NFL. "All-pro!" the girl had exclaimed, pausing for a moment. "Turn around." So Towns knew a celebrated ballplayer, but he would vastly have preferred meeting him in another way. Why couldn't he have run into him, say, in some sporting capacity? The person he knew who boasted the most distinguished credentials was a lady poet who had once bummed around with Ernest Hemingway. Towns felt that this lady was his link to the literary greats of yesteryear. He gave himself high marks for taking her to Chinese restaurants, despite her advanced age. It was a sign of his maturity that he allowed himself to be seen around with a woman who was not exactly a cupcake. But she was hard on him, and made him feel that his behavior was not first-rate and true like that of the literary greats of yesteryear she had once bummed around with. For example, when she ordered fried carp with noodles, her voice was firm, her gaze at the waiter steady, and there was a sense of her having come up with a dish that was first-rate and full of integrity. Whereas, if Harry Towns went for the sea bass with black-bean-and-garlic sauce, she gave him a look of cold steel that said he had done something second-rate and not really true. As he spoke to the waiter, she would crane her head around as if searching the restaurant for some small trace of the honesty and lack of pretense she had experienced in Paris during the Thirties. Hemingway would have picked Towns off as a phony the second he placed such an order, and she was more or less acting in his behalf. So he didn't see her too often. There was a strong chance he fell a little short in the integrity department; he didn't need to have it rubbed in. He sensed that his notion of moving away from waitresses and hookers in the direction of mature women was a sound one, but he did not have much luck with his first tries.

She may not have known he took any, but he saw his wife as someone who would keep the cocaine out of his nose. She would cross her arms and take up a position that would block the hookers and girl-burners, the people who knew about silencers, and the fellows waiting to "go up" from getting at him. And while she was holding them off, he could get back to being a serious man. This included getting involved in television, which he kept describing as a medium that was ready to "step on the gas." He had once said this to the lady poet who had bummed around with Hemingway, and she took it as confirmation of what she had always felt about him, that despite his lip service to Camus and Doctor Johnson, he was really second-rate. Ninth-rate, if you wanted to press her on it. Imagine Hem taking the tube seriously. Or Malcolm Lowry, someone else she had bummed around with, only in Mexico. But he would not have to care about her. If he got his wife back, she would be out of the picture. She would be in there with the coke dealers, part of his past life. There was no way, for example, to team up the lady poet and his wife. Each would think the other second-rate, and you would have a stand-off.

His wife had always said that when and if she ever wanted him back, she would tell him, straight out. So there was a certain amount of risk involved in letting her know he was ready to make the move. She could slap him down. They had an arrangement in which they still went to a few family functions together, her family's and what was left of his. In particular, they went to weddings. These would bring out a certain amount of bitterness in her. During one ceremony, she said, "Big deal. In a couple of years, they'll be fucking other people." Towns couldn't get over the look on her face when she came out with that one. On the other hand, when they danced, after the ceremony, she would hold him in such a way that he could feel a little thrill to her flesh. He had never felt that when they were together. He took that tremulous little shiver to be her way of saying she wanted him back. So, on one occasion, having tested the water, so to speak, he plunged in and said, "Listen . . ." And she said, "I know . . . and I want you to." In what one of his friends had described as "a lightning move with her bishop," she had sold their old house in the country and taken what he saw as a kind of sliced-off apartment in a thickly ethnic, low-rent quarter of the city. It was a slice of an apartment to him in the sense that half of it was outdoors and terraced and the other half was indoors, long and skinny. He imagined himself having to stand sideways all the time to fit into it. But he had visited it, and it had terrific cooking smells in it and a sense of order. Heavy nourishing stews were always bubbling away on the stove; and there were bulletin-board markings, telling when floor shellackers were due. He looked forward to getting involved in those stews. And it would be nice to have some of those bulletin-board notations relate to him. Maybe he could even ink in a few himself. That would mean farewell to coke and egg rolls, except maybe once in a while on the latter. He sublet his own apartment and decided to store his steel and leather furniture rather than sell it. It may be that he was hedging his bets a little on that one. On the other hand, he loved his furniture, and wondered if you were allowed to visit it in storage. He imagined a warehouse fellow taking him in to see it, leaving him alone with it for a while, then coming back to say, "Your time's up, sir." Moving some of it to the sliced-off apartment was out of the question. It would be like bringing a few hookers into his wife's apartment, and he didn't want to do that to her. Even an end table or a plant would be hookers. He waited for a rush of emotion as the movers crated up his furniture, and he said good-bye to his old life, but none came. He thought it would turn up when the apartment was bare and he took his last romantic look at the skyline, the view of the three bridges that had cost him at least an extra hundred a month, but it didn't come then either. When a storage man cut the wires of his telephones and told him to take the actual phones along, because they were worth ten bucks apiece, he got a rush, but just a small one. It was a funny time to have that happen, standing in the bare apartment, holding two strangled phones. But that was the thing about him. He never knew when he was going to be touched. While the storage fellows were wrapping up his glassed-in musical-comedy posters, he went into the bathroom and snorted up the last of his coke. If only the storage fellows knew what he was doing in there. Then he headed for his wife's stews.

The first major event that happened once he had moved in was that his son swiped a giant pencil sharpener from one of the ethnic stores and got traced back to the apartment by a team of detectives. Harry Towns had been out buying some cigars. When he walked in, he saw his teenage son sitting on a kitchen step ladder in handcuffs. Actually, all he saw were the handcuffs. He didn't wait for the story from his wife or the detectives. All he knew was that the handcuffs had to come off. That was worth his life, then and there. Without raising his voice, he communicated this fact to the detectives. There was a good detective and a bad detective, and the good one unlocked them. The bad one, a dead ringer for the French mime stick-up man who was "going up," was breathing heavily from the exertion of getting the cuffs on. Harry Towns had not done any sober reasoning. He could not get his eyes off the handcuffs, and he could not think past them. They had nothing to do with him or anyone that came from him. They were for other people. His family, his father, his uncles were not handcuff people. So how could his son be? Once they were off, Harry Towns calmed down a little. His son didn't say a word, but simply looked at the detectives with what appeared to be gratitude for confirming feelings he had always had about police. Later, Harry Towns would say something to the effect that they were doing their job, but the boy would never forgive them for putting cuffs on him over a sharpener, one he had taken because he had had three years of bum knees and occasionally did things that were a little out of sync. And he had no dad around to keep an eye on him. He would never forgive them, but he also loved them for letting him hate them. Meanwhile, Harry Towns swung into action. This took the form of getting a distinguished attorney with enfeebled kidneys down to the apartment in forty-five minutes. On a weekend. There was talk about booking Towns's son, but there was also a quiet hint from the attorney that there had been an illegal entry; it was settled by everyone agreeing to sit by silently while the bad detective delivered an uninterrupted lecture to the boy about how he shouldn't grab sharpeners that weren't his, since this style of behavior led to major crimes. It was difficult for Towns to sit quietly during the lecture, but he held himself in check. After the talk, the two detectives shook hands all around and went home. The attorney stayed for a brandy, Harry Towns wondering all the while if his kidneys hadn't been further imperiled by the excitement. How could they not have been? He came to the conclusion that this attorney should restrict himself to a calmer form of law. But he did not think it was his province to suggest this.

Harry Towns thought it was certainly lucky he was around for this episode. Otherwise, the boy would have had to remain in the cuffs for a long time. Maybe overnight. He had moved back to his family in the nick of time.

Back at the wedding, Towns's wife had said it would be terrific to get back into one bed again. He was not licking his lips over the prospect, but he was more than willing to go with it. The first time he walked into the bedroom, he saw that she had bought two identical-sized beds and thrown a quilt over them to make it look like one. So technically speaking, it wasn't one bed. And it was more than technical. It meant that someone had to come over to someone else's side. And there was a crevice in the middle. Sometimes he thought of it as a deep one that you could go plunging into, like a skier missing a jump. Later, they would find you at the bottom, crumpled up.

She made love to him in a dutiful way, which he supposed was an advance over their old days together, when for the most part it was no dice. In a court of law, he would have to say she made herself "available" to him. She was "responsible" in bed, he had to give her that. Just as she was responsible in making neat floor-shellacker notations on the kitchen bulletin board. But he couldn't stir up the shiver and thrill he had felt in her flesh during the wedding dances before they got back together. There were a thousand early reasons for this—and sometimes they talked about them until they were blue in the face—but he had his own theory, and it was one he found difficult to discuss. It had to do with the instant they met. When he first saw her, he couldn't speak. She was so beautiful that nothing in his mouth worked. On the other hand, when she got a load of him, her smile, which struck him as being on the perfect side, dropped a little to the right, although she tried bravely to keep it even. The girlfriend who had fixed them up had led her to believe that he had another kind of face. Once again, bravely, she tried to go with what she saw as his "truckdriver" features, but she had clearly been hoping for someone finer looking. Like the cabaret piano player who had been her previous lover. Or would have been, if girls had had lovers in those days. That's where it began, he believed, and that's where it would end. Exhibit A: her face stopped his heart; Exhibit B: he did not look like a cabaret piano player. He didn't care if a massive land army of psychoanalytical giants converged on him with evidence to the contrary, he was sticking to that. It was ironic, too. She was in her forties now, with a new set to her jaw, and if there was anything that stopped his heart, it was her courage in turning herself inside out. Coming out from behind layers of make-up and forgetting about her ankles, which she had always felt were too thick. They were not exactly a favorite masturbatory fantasy of his, but any impartial jury would have found them adequate, if not exactly winners. And they would have had something to say about her throwing over entire decades to fretting about them. But she had cut through the underbrush of her young days, and come out into some kind of clearing. Instead of running off with Greek pilots (the cabaret piano player), she was making floor-shellacker notations on kitchen bulletin boards, whipping up gourmet beef stews, and sneaking in time to help a costume designer on off-Broadway shows. She was dutiful and responsible in bed, and if she had any fleeting concern about her ankles, she held it at just that. She had fought her way out of the Pretty Business. She was really something. It was as if she had taken a handful of tank-town rookies, some overage outfielders, gone out of the franchise for a few authentic hitters, and turned this pick-up crew into a pennant contender. The only trouble was that Harry Towns had lost his interest in baseball.

He did a *Cosmopolitan* magazine thing one night, staying out late with her and checking into a hotel with no luggage. He fed her cocaine (his idea, not *Cosmopolitan*'s) and predictably, asking no questions, she lunged out for it and swore she was reborn. She tore at him, her body pleading, but she could go only so far with it, and at one point, she drew back, holding his cock, as though in mortgage, and asked him to say he would never use it on anyone else. As her part of the bargain, she would take care of it. He asked her if she would please give his cock back, because he didn't feel like making that kind of promise to anyone. He didn't see any need to. It was all very desperate. He wanted to be with someone he didn't have to make that kind of promise to. If and when he found that kind of person, there wouldn't be any need for promises. And it followed he wouldn't go passing it around, either. And what if he did once in awhile? How would it affect Western civilization?

From then on, he stayed on his side of the twin beds that were disguised to look like a double, and never again risked breaking his bones by leaping over the crevice. What he did was switch over to running for a while. There was a track nearby, and after a few months of getting nowhere, being a tired fellow with frail arches, he got good at it. She eagerly pitched in and helped him along. A new bulletin-board notation read: "Wash Harry's sweat suit." She would do anything for him. The only thing she could not do was make believe he had the delicate features of a cabaret piano player. He would waltz out of the sliced-off apartment in his sweat suit, wearing three heavy rings on his fingers that might just as well have been brass knuckles. This was in case anyone in the highly ethnic neighborhood fucked around with him. The biggest challenge was to let young Catholic-high-school runners breeze past him while he kept his pace. There was another type of fellow who would high-kick by in a snotty way, but he knew this style of runner would drop out just as soon as he was around a bend where Towns wasn't able to see him. You couldn't run for miles with those high kicks, and this is what Harry Towns was after. You had to keep your feet low to the ground, almost shuffling. Once, in the early evening, when it was cool, he broke five miles and for a minute or two he felt he could run forever. His chest didn't hurt any more. Watching him from the terrace of the sliced-off apartment, his son said he seemed to be crawling. "I'm shooting for distance," said Harry Towns, "and I'll bet you there isn't one guy in fifty my age can go that far." His son agreed with him on that one, but you could tell he wished his dad would pick up the pace a bit. It was probably embarrassing to have a father crawling around the track with young Catholic

guys zipping past him. Still, Harry Towns loved the running, and burst out of the building each day as if he were
gasping for oxygen. Then he started bouncing around the
track. That was his life: running and stews. Maybe if he
kept running, he could bounce right along to the end of
the line. Running, hot stews, bulletin-board notations,
some writing for television, a medium that was ready to
step on the gas, and out. What was so bad about that?
What was bad was that he saw his life as having a giant
lie buried in the middle of it, one that had to be plucked
out. Once in a while, he would have dinner with a
bodyguard friend of his, and he would say just that—
"There's a lie right in the middle of my life. I have to take
it out." He thought of the flag at Iwo Jima, and the ethni-
cally mixed little band on the poster, who were trying to
drive it into the ground. He imagined that there was a flag
staked between his wife's two beds that were gotten up to
look like one. Instead of the stars and stripes, it had the
word "Lie" printed on it, fluttering in the breeze of the air-
conditioner; unlike the Iwo heroes, it was his obligation to
pull it out of there.

One of the developments that had gotten him back to his
family was the loss of his mother and father, back to
back, his father in particular. When something like that
happened, weren't you supposed to hold on to whatever
you had—your son, your wife, stews? He had done that,
but now another impulse took hold of him—to stop the
shit. To pare himself all the way down to something
clean. To get rid of everything and find out once and for
all if there was anything clean to get down to. That meant
saying good-bye to the doctor he wasn't comfortable with,
and the insurance man he had inherited from his folks,
and the ancient dentist who pinched his gums. And not

writing for television which, let's face it, was not ready to step on the gas. Most of all, it meant setting himself, almost like an Olympic athlete, a fellow from East Germany, so that he got all of his strength concentrated in his legs and his arms and could haul out the lie between the beds.

So he stopped running, and told his wife to hold off on the stew one night because he wanted to talk to her in a restaurant, even though it was in the middle of the week. They picked a restaurant that he didn't think was so romantic, and she did. It went exactly the way it had at the wedding. He said, "Listen . . ." and she covered his folded hands, kissed him, getting back that fragile gently-tissued give to her flesh, and said, "I know." This was some girl. And boy, did he love her now. She had tiny experiential lines around her eyes; she no longer had a summer fragrance to her, or the face that had stopped his heart, but she stopped it another way. He generally switched off when someone said that mature women were like vintage wine, but he had to confess that the comparison applied here. Maybe that's why so many people used it. A favorite kind of film of theirs was one in which the perfect lovers would part at the end, sadly, but with no question that it had to be that way. One of them, usually the girl, would ask forlornly, "Why, Bill?," to which Bill would say, "Because we have to, darling." Then Bill would ship out on a freighter leaving her standing on a dock in Hong Kong. But actually, nobody *knew* why. It was assumed that everyone knew, but nobody did, and that included the trio of screenwriters who had thrown together the script. Maybe the studio heads knew and were keeping it to themselves. From time to time, Harry Towns and his wife would laugh about that kind of picture, and now they were following the same story line. He couldn't put his finger precisely on the reason he was leaving either. He was unhappy, and that was enough for him. This time, when he packed, he took all of his slacks. He went through his bureaus and took along every trace of himself, although he didn't take any more books, since he had the best ones. *His* best ones; he would never have taken *her* best ones. She had come a long way, but she was not about to plunge into *If It Die*. For all of her new perfection, she stood by and watched him pack, saying, more than once, "Are you sure you've got everything?" It would have pleased him more if she had slipped out to shop for health foods. When she wasn't watching him, his son took over. They worked in shifts. A friend of Harry Towns had been trying to move away from his family for fifteen years, always folding in the clutch. One night, when he was packing for the twelve-hundredth time, and was about to crumble again, his son said to him, "Dad, if you go back on yourself, I'll never forgive you." He credited this remark with giving him the strength to get out of there. Harry Towns's son didn't make that type of remark, but he did something better—he looked at his father and hugged him in a way that said he didn't have to worry about cuffs any more. They would never be on him again.

Harry Towns was so anxious to get all his slacks and old bandannas out of there, he almost forgot he had nowhere to take them. He quickly rented the first place they showed him, making sure only that it was a strong departure from the coldness and impersonality of his steel-and-leather apartment, thirty floors above the city. He took one giant room, a kind of studio in a brownstone. It wasn't exactly a bare room, since it had two long smoked-glass mirrors to cover the charm department. It also had a loft that you climbed up to for sleeping. He was worried about crashing through to the sink below, but the landlord assured him it had been built by a Greek who guaranteed that a dozen people could do tempestuous, high-kicking dances up there and it would hold them. Harry Towns didn't pay enough attention to the neighborhood he was in, and it turned out that there was no neighborhood. The apartment was ringed by elegant hotels with carpets out front. Officials in the Commerce Department stayed in these hotels, as well as representatives of Southwest utility companies. If there was a place where you could get a grilled-cheese sandwich, Harry Towns couldn't find it. There were a lot of models out with their dogs, and an Italian hair-styling place that featured extreme and up-to-the-minute cuts, just in from Rome. He couldn't imagine establishing a meaningful relationship with a person who had one of those cuts. From Harry Towns's new window he could see an art gallery and the embassy of a Persian Gulf country. The landlord said the street looked just like Paris, and he had a point there. The smoked-glass mirrors and the art gallery across the street added up to a certain degree of charm. Harry Towns had to admit that. Except that there was no place to get a BLT down. Or a strainer. He got his cold leather and steel furniture out of storage, and it just fit in with the smoked-glass mirrors by an eyelash. It looked a little like he knew what he was doing. It was amazing how much taking *all* his slacks affected him. When he had taken only half his slacks, he was more or less comfortable, but now that he had them all, his stomach fell a little. The first morning away, with all his slacks, he got up early and did a little heartsick running in a park next to the hotels, and wound up in a zoo. It occurred to him that he could have breakfast there, except that the cafeteria wasn't open yet. So he stood opposite the antelope cage while he waited for the breakfast place to start serving. In all his years of knocking around, he had never before taken a good hard look at an antelope, and now he did. What in the hell kind of animal was that? What did they need them for? And, on top of that, he started to feel a little like one. He and the antelopes were both waiting around, kind of directionless, their futures uncertain. He might as well have gotten right in the cage and stood around with them. He had a zoo breakfast, featuring zoo Rice Krispies, zoo milk, and zoo orange juice. The next day he had breakfast in one of the elegant hotels with a crowd of Southwest utility executives planning their pitches for the day ahead. He kept having his breakfasts there, even though he wasn't blending in.

He decided he had better do something fast. Trips had always helped him before, so he did some fast packing and headed West, going deep inside the country, maybe to see some places he hadn't seen before. Copenhagen and Trondheim were out of the question. He had been cut off from his mother and father and family, and he wouldn't be able to stand having the ocean between him and whatever was left. There were a couple of loose ends to take care of which he wound up not taking care of. One was a trip to his father's grave. He knew what would be out there, so he didn't go to see it. It would just be a small rock, and he would feel badly about not having put in a bigger one. And his father would be under it, where he couldn't see him. So why go out there? He took out his father's old-fashioned vest-pocket watch and squeezed it in his hand awhile and saved himself a trip. Everybody old was dead now, except for an aunt in an institution who kept on being alive. That was her main attribute. She looked a little like his father, and if he went to see her he would at least get that out of it, but it would involve taking an awfully long trip, so he passed. He had never been that crazy about her, even though she had let him go through stacks of movie magazines when he stopped off to visit her on his way home from school. She was half-gone when they took her away, and she had to be totally out of her bird now. He didn't see why he had to take a long journey to see his ancient aunt, just because she was alive, resembled his dad, and had once let him flip through back issues of *Modern Screen*. Maybe another and better fellow, more pure in character, would have schlepped out there on that basis, but Harry Towns was not that person, so he took a plane to St. Louis, rented a car there, and headed for unfamiliar towns in the Southwest, ones with great and adventure-filled names.

He drove through Yuma and El Centro and Tucson, stopping at barbeque pits for local color and trying to be amazed and enlightened by packs of bikers who called themselves "The Eternal Drifters." They looked tired from all the drifting, and tended to have bad skin. Towns guessed that if one of them had enough nerve to suggest they stop drifting, they would all quit in a second, because they were on the old side—but so far no one had come forth with this suggestion, and they had to keep at it. Towns felt no urge to tie on with them, even though each pack featured one diamond of a long-haired girl, drifting along with them because no one had told her she was involved in a boring activity. He stopped at a natural preserve called the Salton Sea, forty miles wide, very natural, and empty. It didn't smell that great, but he laid out on a rock, blanketed in stillness, a type of thing he had never done before, and tried to fill himself with a sense of wonder at the vastness of the place. Except that it wasn't that vast. He had been to vaster places. He stopped at a date farm, where the women in charge had little datelike faces, and he ate a lot of date products, shakes, jellies, candies, and special bars that had been made from special offbeat date species, given extra care from birth. He loved dates, but by the time he had his fill, he was nauseated and knew he wouldn't be getting back to them for awhile. The women on the farm had spent all their lives in this work. They looked healthy, robust, and philosophical, although there wasn't one in the bunch who could properly be described as a bundle of mischief. Even though he was still a little nauseated as he drove off, he speculated for a split second on whether he ought to try to move in with them and spend his life in dates.

One of the things Harry Towns was not good at was staying over at someone's house as a guest, and another was looking up people when he was in the neighborhood. But since he was trying new approaches to life, he looked up a Border Patrol man in a nasty little Southwest town called Brawley. The visit tied in slightly with research he was doing on customs and immigration. Harmon, the fellow in question, had been a famous highway patrolman who had gone sweeping off a bridge in pursuit of two young tire thieves, and broken most of his bones. So they shifted him over to the Border Patrol, where he was now famed for his skill at spotting Mexican "illegals" who had gotten as far north as Brawley without being detected. He was eagle-eyed at this, even though he was a little sleepy and his bones were on the soft side. He was one of those sleepy eagle-eyed fellows. He could pick off Mexicans even when they wore sets of diversionary cow hooves, sold to them on the Mexican side. In two hours of bouncing around the outskirts of Brawley with Harmon at the wheel of a Jeep, Towns got to know all he wanted to about Border Patrol work. He liked the sniperscopes that had been developed in Vietnam and could pick off Mexicans in the dark, but that's all he liked about the work. Harmon tried to get him interested in the grid lines of defense the Patrol had set up to ensnarl the errant Mexicans, but it wasn't for Towns. When his new friend told him the agency occasionally took in old guys, Towns let it go by; he might just as well have taken a shot at dates. Harmon had a dutiful Mexican wife, and Towns couldn't help wondering if, one moonlit night, he hadn't spotted her on a grid line wearing cow hooves and kept her for himself. The Mexican wife served them dinner, and when she had dutifully gone off to grind something, Harmon took a few sleepy puffs on his pipe and told Towns about a girl he admired who was living in Brawley and wasn't like the other Brawley people. By the time he had finished telling Towns about her, Towns knew Harmon was in love with this girl but felt that because he was sleepy all the time and his bones were lopsided, there was no way for him to have a shot at her. He worshipped her from a distance, and slipped her regular chunks of his salary, easily finessing these sums past his wife, thanks to the language barrier. "She doesn't have a wicked bone in her body," said Harmon, who, come to think of it, related an awful lot of his thinking to bones. There was an exchange of glances between the two men that said Towns was allowed to meet her and, if it went that way, to fuck her, but he wasn't to hurt her in any way. If he did, Harmon would come after him, in his sleepy, soft-boned style.

The girl came over to meet Towns in his Brawley hotel,

and he immediately went into a nonstop recitation about the back-to-back loss of his folks and how he had broken up his family and wasn't sure which way he was heading. He hadn't expected to tell her all that, but he got it in with one burst before she said a word. She wasn't so much listening as waiting for him to stop, and when he did she went for him as though he were a lobster dinner and she hadn't eaten in a week. She seemed to have been waiting for someone to come into Brawley and say he had lost his folks, busted up his family, and was rudderless. This was a fine stroke of luck for Harry Towns, but it was also puzzling because, appearance-wise, she was the kind of girl he generally wrote off, right at the top, as being for other people. He tended to think this kind of girl was out of his league. He kept saying he would get around to girls like this at some later point. After he had won some kind of Outstanding Citizen's award. She was blonde and had a slender, long-legged, playful kind of New England body. He had seen this kind of girl with other men, fellows with massive rolling banks of attractively disordered hair and Juan-les-Pins suntans. He generally spotted them leaving restaurants. Sometimes he got a defective version of this type of girl, one who was old or had a speech impediment; but until he got to Brawley, he had never had the real McCoy. That was supposed to be coming up later, except that later seemed to be now. Right there in Brawley. What did she see in him? That Harmon must have given him some introduction. She couldn't have been more than twenty-four; and she didn't have a limp or a skin condition that was immediately discernible. She was *it*, a flirtatious, prime, government-inspected, New England-finishing-school, horse-jumping, delicious-smelling, blue-eyed, absolutely A-Number-One specimen of blondeness who, to cap it all off, delivered the goods. Ten minutes after they met she was sucking him off, using inventive little finishing-school tricks, as if she were terrified of missing the mark and being dismissed with a bored wave of Harry Towns's hand. Maybe Brawley had something to do with it. All they had there were Harmon and fellows who worked for feed companies. Not too many screenwriters passed through Brawley, even depressed rudderless ones.

He tried his best to settle in and enjoy her, but the missing pieces kept nagging at him. He had told her straight out the way he was, not feeding her pâté, caviar, chilled white wine, and shoving cocaine in her nose, his usual style. Instead, he came right out and gave her rudderless. Maybe that's what it was. Maybe if he did that more often (went straight to rudderless), he could be one of the fellows seen leaving restaurants with this type of girl. Her lovemaking had a stop-and-start style to it. Each time they finished up one section, she would sit up with her back arched, put her fingers to her lips as if she were a secretary who had forgotten an important memo, then shrug it off and return for the next section. He liked those pert secretarial pauses, particularly after he mastered the rhythm of them. He could not imagine ever getting tired of them.

That first night, he walked her back to her small ranch house, which was hair-raisingly neat, and found another missing piece, except that it was a terrific one. She had a little girl who was an exact replica of herself, with a Latin overlay that gave the New England style some seasoning. "She's awful," said her mother, as she hopped right up on Harry Towns's lap. "She goes around all day with no pants." As if Harry Towns had to be told that. He knew that the second she hopped up there, even though he wasn't used to little girls. He did freight train imitations and coin tricks, quickly exhausting his repertoire but she stayed on his lap anyway. She would have stayed on there for a few weeks if her mother hadn't pried her off. The Latin seasoning came from her father, a product of Rio nobility, who had sworn he was coming to get her, using bribes and guns if necessary. For about a week, Harry Towns forgot all about his past and his roots and got right into the middle of this situation, seeing himself as a fellow whose obligation it was to stand between the two females and the South-of-the-Border nobleman who had beaten them both up, causing them to flee Rio and hide in Brawley. That father was banned from the States for poor moral character; but if he ever bribed his way ashore and made his way inland, tracking his old family down, Harry Towns felt confident he would know how to deal with him. In the event that he brought along Rio guns, there was always Harmon to help out. He sympathized with the Latin for wanting to have his daughter back, but there was no excuse for him slamming the two of them around. Harry Towns gave his new friend seven hundred dollars as a step toward putting some legal distance between herself and the Rio man. She protested an awful lot about accepting the money, but he got her to take it anyway. He was never in any doubt that she would. And it was money he needed.

The yellow-haired New England girl was a bit like a high-keyed filly; each night he stroked her and made love to her, often just to calm her down. They made love on a rug in front of a fireplace, even though it was much too hot for that in Brawley. It was because she was romantically inclined that she felt she had to bring the fireplace into play. After one of her secretarial pauses, instead of plunging on to the next lovemaking sequence, she jumped up and decided they all ought to sweep off to Bali. Only she wasn't kidding. Before the Rio nobleman had developed a poor moral character and started smacking her in the head, they used to do things like that—sweep off to Bali or Villefranche. The whole fun of it was to do it on impulse. Harry Towns was charmed by her jumping up and down naked, saying, "Let's do it, let's do it," but he wasn't one of those people. He was more deliberate.

She suggested that they both refer to his cock as "Pepe," and that's another move he didn't much care for. "It's just part of my body," he said. "There's no need to give it a name." He really disappointed her on that one; she made many efforts to get the name to stick, which he fended off. Greeting him at the door, she would ask, "How's Pepe today?" To which he would say, "Look, I'm willing to go with you on a lot of things, but I'm just not buying Pepe." He would have bet anything that the Rio man went in for that. That's probably where the idea originated. The Rio man probably wouldn't dream of going around the corner unless he had at least three names festooned on his dick.

Another thing he wouldn't do was stay over at her place, although he was unable to explain why. Even if it was four in the morning, he went back to his Brawley hotel, and not because his room was quaint. Brawley was a town without quaintness. All he could come up with to support his position was the behavior of the late Lenny Bruce, who had hundreds of affairs but never stayed over at a girl's house. He had a feeling the New England girl would not take comfort in that so he didn't bother telling her about the great stand-up comic's predilections.

After a few weeks in Brawley, he started to get a little

lonely, even though he wasn't sure what he was lonely for. He missed his son, but he knew the boy was all right, so he didn't miss him that much. Did he miss his new apartment, the one that was in the middle of regally carpeted hotels? How could he miss his mother and father back East, when they were underground? Did he miss his father's pocket watch and the picture of both his folks, which for some reason he didn't frame but kept tucked inside an Italian sportshirt? Was he lonely for the bodyguards and stewardesses? Maybe it was Brawley that was getting to him, a place that was built for driving through but definitely not for staying in. Each little wave of loneliness got the girl more keyed up; she had terrifically keen antennae for loneliness. Whenever a wave of it broke against Harry Towns, she popped her fragrant little daughter onto his lap and the child clung to Harry Towns's neck. One night, when he was lying in the blonde girl's bed, she slipped her sleeping little daughter under the covers with him and said she was going out to get some fried chicken breasts. They were a favorite of his and they weren't bad in Brawley. While she was gone, Harry Towns hugged the little girl, who was sucking her thumb, and gave her quite a few licks between her legs. It was only later that he considered the possible consequences, that instantly upon hitting her teens, she would take on the entire male and female population of St. Tropez, including dogs and pet ocelots, in pursuit of those mysterious comatose primal licks. Still, at the moment, it would have taken a squadron of highly motivated commandos to hold him back. She pressed herself toward him, and seemed to keep on sleeping. After he had done this, he knew he would have no need ever to do it again. He wasn't going to be one of those fellows who gets rounded up every time there is a local sex crime. The experience just wasn't apocalyptical. But he had to work it in once and get it out of the way. When her mother came back with the fried chicken breasts, Harry Towns said, "All I did was hug her." The mother's smile had a mischievous wrinkle to it as she scooped up the little girl and slipped her back in her own bed. "I'll just bet," she said. At the moment, he felt the Rio nobleman ought to be greeted at the docks with a brass band and Harry Towns shipped out of the country. But he also saw that he had been set up. It would have been different if he had tiptoed over to the girl's cot in the dead of night and leaned in for some furtive licks. But her own mother had slipped her in there with him. She could only have been giving Harry Towns a sneak preview of what it could be like if he stayed with the two of them. As the mother declined, which had to be quite a ways off, her daughter would be ripening in the sun, blonde, fragrant, Continentally seasoned, ready to go on stage in her mother's place.

Still, he backed off. One night, a wave of sadness, bigger and more serious than the previous ones, washed over Harry Towns.

"Can't you see that you're unhappy?" she said.

"I know that," he said.

"And you're depressed."

"I know that. Do you think that's what makes unhappy people happy? Telling them that they're not happy?"

"But you're so miserable."

She was a lovely woman, with many fine qualities, but dealing out insightful therapy was not her strong suit. He felt a sudden flash of kinship with the high-born Rio man. He didn't know quite how to leave, so one night, in order to indicate to her that their relationship had reached a shaky stage, he drove his fist through the mantel. It was a cheaply constructed Brawley-designed structure, so his fist went through easily, skinning his knuckles but not breaking them. It began as a gesture, but it turned into a genuine rage that didn't subside as he drove back East. Waiting for him was a series of letters from the girl, setting forth painstaking analyses of the precise quality of her love for him. One of them said she had once been in love with him, but now she just loved him. In the second letter, she told him to forget the first one. What she really meant was that it was impossible to love and not be loved, so her love had shifted to a different plateau, not higher or lower, but more or less off to the side, although not beyond reach. He didn't read the third letter, because he didn't know what the fuck she was talking about. And he was having dreams about rugged substantial-looking men with an arm or a leg missing. As far as he could recall, these were his first severed-limb dreams, and he was all in favor of canceling the series.

For lack of a better plan, he reverted to his old style, getting involved with a black, thickly gummed new form of cocaine and a nest of girls who went in and out of drug rehabilitation centers. Each one was in her early twenties, going on forty-five, but temporarily pretty. He had to wait for them to sign out on passes in order to get at them. At least they weren't Pepe girls. He developed a small lesion on his penis, which he let slide; shortly thereafter, two of the girls phoned and reported raging brush-fire infections in their bodily orifices. A friend of his, who ran into one, said, "What did you do to Holly? She looks as if she spent two years in the Mekong Delta." They had a chuckle about this, although when Harry Towns walked off, he thought to himself that he must be some sonofabitch for doing that to Holly.

Going back into cocaine, especially black gummed coke, after a long time away, was like diving into a pool without checking the water level. Harry Towns cracked his head on the bottom. One night, in his loft with a freshly healed rehabilitation girl, he went into a deep coma, which was oddly pleasant until he realized he was not going to have an easy time climbing out of it. The drug-center girl brought him a great soup bowl of coffee which helped Harry Towns get to his feet and over to the new doctor he had switched to. This man took care of people in the communications field and had once smacked a Secretary of State and gotten away with it. Towns liked knowing that about him. The new man said he had an illness of the blood which would keep him exhausted for months. Harry Towns had been living in fear of big-league diseases; he grabbed the blood problem and ran like a thief. But it was big league enough. He felt as if his bones had turned to sponge. Now he knew what Harmon went through, although at least the Brawley man had the Border Patrol to distract him. It was all Harry Towns could do to answer the phone, so he didn't answer it. He named himself Sergeant Spongecake, although he was careful not to say that to anyone. If the little girl from the Southwest ever visited him, he might say it to her. His wife wanted to run over with nourishing stews, but that would have started up some machinery he wanted to keep idle so he held her off.

Once again, illness had come to his rescue. It had always pinned him by the shoulders and forced him to give himself a once-over. It did this time, too. The doctor told Harry Towns that this was the kind of illness it was best to ignore. Just hang in there, don't do anything preposterous, and eventually it would peter out. It was a little hard to ignore. Following those instructions would be like living in a tiny apartment with an Irish wolfhound and pretending it wasn't there. But Harry Towns set out to ignore his illness as aggressively as possible. Once in a while, he would get a spasm of energy. During one of them, he stood up and put on a record, not for a stewardess or a drug rehab girl, but just for himself. With no coke to season the music. When was the last time he had done something like that? He read a few Civil War books, and started *Middlemarch,* giving it a new, more mature reading. He read it to find out what was in it, not to get through it and have a notch on his belt. When he was strong enough to walk, he took another look at the neighborhood. He found out it wasn't all regal hotels and Persian Gulf embassies. Salted in among them was a tiny dry-cleaning store and a delicatessen where you could get corned-beef sandwiches. They were on the regal and slick side, but they were a start. Once the delicatessen fellows saw that you were a regular, they would make non-menu French toast for you, sneaking it out clandestinely so that the transient utility execs didn't get wind of it. He bought an extension cord in a store that was only nine blocks away. He just hadn't checked the neighborhood thoroughly the first time. Tiny little stores were stuck away in it like raisins in his mother's rice pudding. He used to have to wade through vast sections in order to ferret out the little black treasures. (Why hadn't she put in more raisins? Certainly it wasn't the cost. Perhaps she was teaching him endurance and the joys that came from persistence of effort.) In any case, the neighborhood was like one of his mother's old rice puddings. He knew that if he hopped in a cab, within five minutes he could find anything from Ukrainian dancers to figs from the Negev, but it was important to establish some kind of beachhead right next to his apartment. A home. He couldn't find a stoop that you could sit out on and watch the world go by, but he made friends with his landlord, a distributor of adventurously designed lamps who lived in the apartment above and the one below. The landlord made no bones about his plans to snare on Towns's studio once his lamp business caught fire. Towns disarmed him by handing him an ancient bottle of brandy. He didn't do this for any personal gain, but the startled landlord became drenched with sweat and fired off a year's extension on the lease, presenting it to Harry Towns on the spot. As another present, he confided that he was part Oriental, and on his third marriage, but not to tell anybody.

When Harry Towns started to feel a little better, he still didn't answer the phone. If a fellow from his old life dropped by, he would arrange himself in a wan position and say, "It's an amazing disease. You think you're making progress and the next day you're back at the starter's gate." He wasn't making that one up either. He said he felt just like a Victorian girl—in a decline. His underworld friends didn't follow him on that one. The illness was a wonderful protection against his old style, and he worked it for all it was worth. The cocaine fell into some perspective, too. A haggard, drug-consumed friend came by to say a girl he was living with had suddenly pulled up stakes and, with no warning, lit out for Oklahoma. Towns's friend dealt with this blow by getting himself an ounce of "girl," the latest name for coke, and taking it to bed with him, staying there with it for three days. It sounded awful to Towns, the loneliest story he could remember hearing. He had handled things that way himself and didn't want to handle them that way anymore. He would not sign an affidavit on this point—it was a terribly alluring force—but he felt he had put cocaine behind him. No doctor had so much as hinted at this, but somehow he connected it up with his illness. It was a scary kind of disease in that there were no rewards for good behavior. Let's say you slept twelve hours straight; you were liable to wake up feeling you needed a little nap. He blamed this state of affairs on the coke, whether it was the coke's fault or not. If someone dropped by with a fistful of it, he would be hard pressed not to take a little taste. He had to admit that. But he felt confident he would not be hunting it down anymore.

One day he helped a girl back from a tiny grocery store with her packages. She came up to his apartment, wriggling and squirming and throwing out her breasts, and said she would like to be Harry Towns's friend, since she was a neighbor and it would be a waste not to be. He said fine, except that she would have to stop doing that with her tits. Otherwise, there would be no basis for a friendship. It would be the same old thing. She seemed relieved to hear this, and let her breasts settle down. And they did become friends, a breakthrough for Harry Towns. He developed a few arrangements like this, girls he wasn't sleeping with, although he did not want this pattern to get out of hand. It was a wrench for him, but he felt he was on the right track. Maybe he would get around to sleeping with them and maybe he wouldn't. There was fun in going either way. And it was a pleasure not to have all that pressure to deal with.

He fixed up his apartment. He did not stock it with

priceless art treasures of the world, but he made sure that everything he picked out was something he liked. If he saw that a napkin holder was not going to give him any pleasure, he kept hunting for one that would. He threw out his glass and mirrored wall decorations. In some wild and circuitous turn of logic that had once made sense to him, he had felt they would be an aid in getting stewardesses to whip off their clothes. A friend had once described his old apartment as looking like an airport lounge. Maybe that was the connection. He bought some plants and took terrific care of them, pleased when they didn't die right off and loving it each time a new little shoot appeared. Once in a while, he would stand back and take a look at his apartment and wonder if it threw off the impression that an interesting fellow lived in it. He thought it probably did, but he couldn't tell for sure. He bought things like Swiss cheese and noodle soup and Crisco, and even weighed in one day with a head of lettuce. Each and every item was nonseductive. And all of this made him feel less rudderless.

He began to feel a faint shiver of the possibilities that were now open to him. He might meet a sweet and easygoing girl he wanted to be with, and if he did, he would even close an eye if she wanted to call his cock "Pepe." She could call it "Arturo" if he felt comfortable with her, although the kind of girl he had in mind wouldn't. In any case, there was no rush on that. He could now go to places like Sofia, although he was seasoned enough to know that such trips were not going to do the trick for him. The main thing was he could go there without having to report in to anyone. For the first time in his life, the only one he had to check in with was Harry Towns. (And there really *was* a reason to go to Sofia. What good was the city if you didn't go to it? It was a waste of thousands of years of civilization and an extremely complex culture. A wasted city.) Or how about doing ten years of hard work? What was wrong with that plan? Non-bodyguard friends, no coke, girls he was friends with, girls he slept with, girls he did both with, and, on occasion, no girls. Or all of the above. Was there any flaw in that attack?

Before he got too ambitious, he had to get his health back. He was not about to recommend it to friends, but he had come up with a remarkable illness and had to admire its ingenious turns. Between spells of weakness, he would suddenly be filled with great foaming cascades of energy, during which he would construct myths, fables, encyclopedic films and novels—what seemed at the time to be ground-breaking theories of time and existence. He took a few notes glancing at them when he got weak again. Some held up. During the wild periods, he would feel frustrated that there weren't typewriters that could keep pace with his output, that a hundred people weren't at his disposal to dispatch his work to the outside world, that he didn't have twenty lives in which to get all of it done. He was no judge, of course, but he didn't *feel* deranged. He just had all this energy and his mind kept swirling. These bursts took a physical turn, too. One day he snapped a handgrip together one hundred and seventy-five times, besting his old record of ninety. He made a breakthrough in running, seven nonstop miles, the full circumference of the nearby park, and seriously considered taking off after Frank Shorter, a man known to relatively few but considered by Harry Towns to be the world's most remarkable athlete. His feat amounted to having run twenty-six five-minute miles, a physiological impossibility, Shorter himself conceding that the body did not store enough caloric energy for the last six miles, which had to be done on Zen. Marathon running was considered an "old man's sport," most champions being men over thirty. Shorter was all the more remarkable for having smashed the record at twenty-five. The great athlete trained twice a day. What if Towns were to do the same and sneak in an extra midnight session? If Shorter did the last six miles on meditation, Towns would go into a trance for the final twelve. Then Towns dropped the idea. He could see that he was being carried away. And besides, is that what he really wanted to do with his life? He switched over to the idea of a publicized jog through the city's highest crime area. Mayoralty candidates could join him if they dared. He would take his last few dollars and announce this jog in a daily newspaper. It was *his* city. He had grown up in it. It was incomprehensible to him that he couldn't take a stroll down certain streets. So he would jog through a series of blocks known as "Homicide Row" at midnight, unprotected, giving every crazy person in the city a clean shot at him. He would do this out of love. But who would believe him? No matter how you sliced it, it came out sounding like a publicity stunt. Although what was he publicizing? His new apartment? His soft bones? Harry Towns, the scenarist, a writer, for the most part, of turkeys? He dropped that idea, too. Part of the reason for his abandonment of the notion was that he was scared shitless.

And then he would get weak again, propping himself up on a pillowed couch, his arms hanging limp, fingers touching the carpeting. Normally, Harry Towns ignored his internal machinery and simply pushed on. Now he wondered for the first time in his life about the source of his strength, such as it was. Doctors had recently made news in the *Times* with a table that allotted points to a person for each of life's personal disasters. Loss of a spouse was worth ninety, a physical illness seventy-two, a job gone up in smoke eighty-five. And so on. Adding up his own setbacks over the past year, Harry Towns, with dead folks, bones gone soft, a shattered family, and grave financial setbacks, broke the bank at three hundred. According to the table, it was a safe prediction that he would currently be found strait-jacketed at Matteawan, staring blankly at the walls. Yet here he was, at one moment foaming with energy, at another surprised and impatient at being depressed and a bit scattered. One night, a producer, renowned for forcing a long list of film workers into nervous collapses, got annoyed at Harry Towns and said he would see to it that he never worked again. Gripping a restaurant table with one hand and feeling the heat of his own eyes as they burned into the other man's, Towns said, "Don't threaten me." To Towns's surprise the producer, toupee slipping over one ear, said, "All right, but whatever you do, please don't yell at me." Where did Harry Towns come up with this strength? Short years back, in the only job he had ever held, he had gone into paroxysms of fear whenever the boss's secretary phoned and said, "Mr. Baldwin wants to see you." Why was he suddenly able to back down the Baldwins? With soft bones. And no money. And no family. And dead folks. Sitting in the park one day, a couple struck up a conversation with him. The man, a former film actor, had eyes that couldn't be fixed, pinballing wildly in his head. Towns assumed this was a result of years of being fucked, literally and figuratively, by studio executives. The girl, attractive, great-breasted, was the daughter of a man who had set up multimillion-dollar foundations dedicated to curing public ills. Seemingly attracted by Harry Towns's ease and calm—he was alone, reading a news magazine, apparently comfortable with himself—the couple clung to him, the girl finally saying, in desperation, "You've been with us awhile and gotten a hint of the way we are. Do you think we should stay together?" Normally, Towns would have rejected this authority. But this time, he considered carefully and said, "If you have to ask . . ." Who knows, it may have been the wrong thing to say. But what was he supposed to be, a trained therapist? They certainly did want to hear something from him. The actor's eyes kept pinballing wildly; the girl nodded with a knowing curl of a smile, and they went off, with what ostensibly was Harry Towns's nugget. What interested him was the way they had been drawn to him. Out of an entire parkful of people. He was some person to ask about staying together. Then again, maybe he wasn't such a bad choice. Maybe he could do things like that, too. Harry Towns, a latecomer in the guru game. Wouldn't that be something.

How had he suddenly come up with all this meat on his bones? Had he borrowed some of his dead parents' flesh? That was certainly an unattractive way to put it. But wasn't it possible he had now taken into himself some of his mother's brashness and ferocity, his father's ability to bend in turmoil, like bamboo, and not crack in half? Until the hurricane died down. Some of Harry Towns's own material had been sprinkled in, and who knows—if each man were more than the product of what filtered through him in a lifetime, then perhaps ancient legend, myth, and wisdom ran through his genes, too. If this were true, didn't his composition make Harry Towns a pasted-up man, ready to fall apart if someone struck exactly the right chord, tapped him along one of his seams? He preferred to think of himself as some kind of strong, functioning mutation of a man. Could you get along if you were one of those? Have a few laughs? His guess was that you could. Still, if such were the case, why did he need someone else around? Why the hunt for sweet and easygoing girls? If a man were possessed of sufficient life force, why did the magazines keep insisting on a "partner," for "real fulfillment," in order to "complete oneself." Why couldn't he go right ahead and be an island, after all, with visiting days on Sunday, or perhaps none at all? Did he require a mirror? To show him he was good? If Harry Towns was good and knew it, why did he need a mirror for verification? Answer him that one.

Meanwhile, setting islands and mirrors aside for the moment, there were shards of loneliness to contend with, some unaccountable, others easy to pinpoint. At an Italian restaurant where Harry Towns ate alone one night, a man from a nearby table approached and said, "Three of us were admiring your shirt. We never saw a shirt like that and wanted to tell you that." Towns thanked the man and said his wife had picked it out. He knew that if he traveled the earth ten times over, he would never run across someone who could pick things out the way she could. He suddenly remembered her style of swimming (they had taken an awful lot of vacations—probably to change the unchangeable)—fast, light, immaculate, and with a delighted smile. He could go on with the list, but it wasn't profitable. So he felt bad for the rest of the dinner and then he was all right again. Despite the high risk of sudden loneliness, Harry Towns, for the most part, preferred to eat dinner alone. For the time being, that's the way he wanted it.

There were still the sudden shockers to deal with. One night, an old bum shuffled out of an alley, called Towns "Nickel Nuts," then shuffled away. Why did he have to do that? Towns would often size up an athlete or a cop and wonder what his chances would be against the fellow. But he was afraid of old bums. They might pull some old-bum trick on you. With an old-bum contraption. Something they had picked up in Singapore. On another occasion, he stopped to listen to a steel band in the park. A Spanish transvestite requested "My Yiddishe Mama," then winked at Towns and said, "For you, baby." Astonishingly, Towns was moved by the band's Latin rendition of the senti- mental melody. Sudden, erratic behavior. And there was another area that was even more uneasy for Harry Towns. The girl from Brawley had given him an animal- skin bracelet and made him swear he would never take it off. Dutifully, Towns had worn it, even after he had put her out of his mind, figuring why fuck around, it will fall off eventually anyway. One day, many months later, she called and said she was passing through, could she drop by and say hello? Harry Towns said yes, of course, and hung up. At that moment, the bracelet fell from his wrist. Naturally and of its own accord. What were the odds against that happening? A trillion to one? Previously, when a person asked Harry Towns his sign, he would consider the conversation finished and the person, too. Did he now want to open that can of peas? He decided he didn't—but it was up there on the shelf, grinning at him—slyly insisting on a confrontation.

For all of his new fragments of insight, Harry Towns flailed around and sought out ways he could be hurt. There were fewer of them than ever before. His mother and father were underground, so they couldn't get him there. The IRS could do just so much damage. There was his son, of course, and the second he thought of the boy, he knew they had him. One day, during one of the weak times, he started to cry about losing his boy suddenly. When Harry Towns was young, he remembered crying a lot, being ashamed of it, and wondering if he was ever going to get past bursting into tears at the drop of a hat. He was positive he was an older crier than any boy on the East Coast. He remembered stopping just before he left for college—as he saw it, just in the nick of time. Now he was back at it again. In his forties. Was he going to keep crying all the way through? Until they carted him off? It was a possibility.

At the moment, the tears related exclusively to his boy. If he could just see to it that nothing happened to him. On his own behalf, there wasn't much he could do about holding off major convulsions such as blindness and impotence. And of course, if he came up with cancer, his goose was cooked. But he made a promise to himself to work on a fallback position, even if he wound up with one of those. Despite a recent turn in that direction, Harry Towns tried to avoid dealing out advice to anyone, but he was convinced that every man had an obligation to do at least that. Both his mother and father had died with enormous grace and lack of selfishness—never mind raging against the night—and don't think that didn't give Harry Towns an advantage. He would take that against any inheritance you could dream up. Which is not to say he had it made. That the world was going to be his oyster. One night he bought a supermarket ready-roasted chicken and, in the course of eating it, plucked out the wishbone. It was the first time he had ever found himself holding both ends. This gave him a heady, uncertain feeling, but there was some pleasure to it and only the tiniest wisp of loneliness. It would be fun having someone on the other end—who could argue forcefully against that?—but there were pluses in having both ends for himself. All bracelet coincidences to the contrary, Harry Towns remained a man who wouldn't touch a symbol with a ten-foot pole. But how was he going to let that one go by?

He had no idea of how he was going to fare, although he was first on line in the curiosity department when it came to finding out. He sensed he ought to do the following things: go to Sofia, or places like it (with modest expectations); keep an eye out for a sweet and easygoing girl (what did he have to lose?); try like hell not to get hit with a brick. Treat each human being he came across with generosity—until such time as he found reason not to. That last one was vital to Harry Towns. And it didn't mean falling all over people, either.

He felt that if he made a strong effort to do each of these things, he had a chance of coming out all right. In Vegas terms, he was even tempted to give himself a slight edge.

A Note on the Type

This book was set in a typeface called Primer, designed by Rudolph Ruzicka for the Mergenthaler Linotype Company and first made available in 1949. Primer, a modified modern face based on Century broadface, has the virtue of great legibility and was designed especially for today's methods of composition and printing. Primer is Ruzicka's third typeface. In 1940 he designed Fairfield, and in 1947 Fairfield Medium, both for the Mergenthaler Linotype Company.

The book was composed, printed, and bound by American Book–Stratford Press, Inc., New York, New York. Typography and binding design by Carole Lowenstein.